Aberdeenshire '
'hrdeens

A Legacy of Secrets

(Book 4: An Irish Family Saga)

Sequel to 'A Turning of the Tide'

by

Jean Reinhardt

Historical Fiction

D1077534

1969222

'Your hunger for rectitude
blossoms into rage
the hot tears of mourning
never shed for you before
your twisted measurements
the agony of denial
the power of unshared secrets.'

From the poem <u>*Inheritance – His*</u>
by Audre Lorde

FT
Pbk

Dedication

To RoseAnne who may write a book
herself one day.

Copyright

Title book: A Legacy of Secrets

Author book: Jean Reinhardt

Text copyright © 2015 Jean Reinhardt

Cover illustration copyright © 2015 Jean
Reinhardt

Self-publishing

jeanreinhardt@yahoo.co.uk

ALL RIGHTS RESERVED. This book contains
material protected under International and
Federal Copyright Laws and Treaties. Any
unauthorized reprint or use of this material is
prohibited. No part of this book may be
reproduced or transmitted in any form or by
any means, electronic or mechanical, including
photocopying, recording, or by any information
storage and retrieval system without express
written permission from the author/publisher.

This is a work of fiction; names, characters,
places, brands, media and incidents are the
product of the author's imagination or are used
fictitiously. James, Mary and Catherine
McGrother are ancestors of the author, however
their story in this book is fictitious.

CHAPTER ONE

"No good will come of this," Patrick said to his companions. "I'm not here to take part in a riot. This was supposed to be a peaceful rally."

Two of the men agreed with him and the trio turned their backs to the impassioned speaker, John De Morgan, a radical agitator with Marxist views. He was standing on the steps of the Market Cross in Stockton, dodging missiles as he delivered his speech to thousands of people. To make matters worse, a number of unruly local youths had pushed their way into the crowd, inviting trouble.

Used to the hard physical labour of quarry work, Patrick and his companions were broad shouldered men, well able to cut a path through the heaving mass packed tight around them.

Some pushing and shoving had broken out at random among the crowd and a loud hissing and booing could be heard, as the Stockton police made their presence known. Reinforcements had been sent for by telegram and when the officers from Middlesbrough arrived they had their cutlasses drawn. By the time Patrick and his companions had forced their way from the centre of the crowd, sporadic fighting was taking place between some of the marchers and those who were antagonistic towards them and their cause.

As the speeches were brought to an abrupt end, the crowd began to move towards the Victorian Bridge, spilling over into South Stockton, where even more rioting took place. Patrick could see a man in the distance on horseback, who appeared to be leading the marchers. He rode into what looked like a mass of flying fists and caps.

"Who's that on the horse?" asked Patrick.

"That's one of the organizers. It looks as if he's trying to break up a fight."

"Good luck to him, I'm not waiting around to get arrested," Patrick changed direction, pitting himself against the flow of marchers, his two friends close on his heels.

Many of those taking part in the rally were of the same mind as Patrick and had already left the street. This helped to thin out the edges making it easier for them to break free of the crowd. From the roof of a nearby building a rock was thrown, catching Patrick on the side of the head and he sank to his knees. Instantly, more missiles followed and the men tried to shield themselves as they dragged their unconscious friend to the safety of a narrow laneway.

"What happened?" asked Patrick, coming round on the rain-soaked cobblestones.

"Some young blackguards on a rooftop are slinging rocks at the crowd. I've half a mind to go up there and knock their heads together," said one of the men.

"Best leave them to it, anyone with an ounce of sense will be doing the same as ourselves and heading for home," Patrick replied.

The rain beat down for most of that cold December day and by the time he arrived at his muddy street, Patrick was soaked to the skin and frozen to the bone.

"You'll catch your death. Get out of those wet clothes," Catherine pulled a sodden cap from her husband's head, revealing a large gash on his temple.

"Now don't go fretting about it," Patrick winced as he touched the wound. "It looks worse than it is. I was only knocked out for a few seconds."

"Knocked out? I told you there would be trouble. There's always trouble at those rallies. Now look at the state of you. Will you never learn, Patrick Gallagher?

As Catherine tended his cuts, placing a cold wet flannel on a rapidly forming bump, Patrick told her about his eventful day.

"There were thousands there, as many as ten thousand I'll wager. I've never been in a crowd that big. I was excited and fearful all at the same time."

"It would have served you better to accompany your wife and children to Mass. This is what you get for your sins," chided Catherine.

"Well, I'll tell it in confession, if it makes you feel any better. Did you keep me some food, or am I to be sent to bed early without supper for my penance?" Patrick gave his wife a mock frown.

Catherine could never stay angry at her husband for long. She dished up a bowl of stew from a pot on the small stove that Patrick had salvaged from a derelict building. It had made all the difference to their tiny damp home, helping to dry out the air. Opening the door to the only other room in the house, Catherine peered into the darkness.

"I'll leave the door ajar, the children have been coughing all evening. I've given them some elixir but we had best keep our voices low so as not to disturb their sleep, Patrick."

"It's living in these back to backs that has them sick so often. We should move, Catherine. There are better houses not too far from here."

"The rents are too high. We would never be able to save a penny or buy decent food. No, we can't afford a better house, unless you agree to me finding employment. The bit of sewing I get doesn't amount to much."

"What, and have your father say I cannot support his daughter? Never."

"Then will you please consider Maggie's offer of a place to stay?" asked Catherine.

"Have you lost your senses, woman. Do you think your father and myself could live in the same parish? He cannot stand the sight of me, and that was plain for all to see the last time he was over. Besides I have work here, most days at least."

Patrick was referring to James and Mary's last visit to see their newest grandchild, his two year old daughter. She had been given her maternal grandmother's name but was called Maisie by the family.

"If you feel crowded in this house at present, it's soon to become even smaller. I'm with child again," Catherine delivered her news as if she was remarking on the wet day outside.

Patrick spluttered on a mouthful of watery stew.

CHAPTER TWO

"Tell Maggie our good news," Mary said in a loud voice.

"Catherine is coming home, isn't that grand, Maggie?" said James.

Mary frowned at her husband, "What he meant to say was Catherine and *Patrick* are coming home, to stay. Isn't that great news? They are hoping to stay with you for a wee while, until Patrick has work got."

"My hearing isn't so bad you have to shout every word at me. Of course they can stay here, for as long as they care to," Maggie glared at Mary before turning to her brother. "Does that mean you've forgiven the poor lad for having the cheek to marry your daughter, James?" There was no response and Maggie huffed. "I thought as much, seeing as you still haven't forgiven me for encouraging him."

"Ah would you stop with your old nonsense. Sure he put that behind him long ago. Isn't that so?" Mary shot a warning glance at James.

"Of course I have. What's done is done. I may not welcome him with open arms but I'll not turn him away either."

"That's very considerate of you, James. I'm sure Patrick will be honoured by your half-hearted attempt to welcome him to the family."

James stood and fixed his cap firmly onto his head. His sister had always been able to get under his skin, in a way that not even his wife had managed to do.

"Well, that's all he can expect, for now at least. Maybe he'll grow on me the longer he's here. Does that cheer you up at all?" James glared down at Maggie.

"Would you look at the face on that, Mary? Keep it away from your hens or they'll stop their laying. Even his beard is in a tizzy."

Both women laughed heartily as James's hand instinctively flew to his chin. He looked disparagingly at each of them before turning his back and heading out through the open door.

"The two of ye are as bad as each other, behaving like that," admonished Mary. "He'll be sour for the day."

"Ah, James doesn't harbour ill feelings for long, except where young Patrick Gallagher is concerned. It's a blessing they'll be living with me and not under his nose in his own house. Mind you, they could be fishing together on the same boat, have you considered that?" asked Maggie.

The thought had never seemed of much significance to Mary until that moment and her face clouded over. She considered the situation before responding.

"James is not a foolish man, he knows better than to bring quarrels out to sea, but Patrick is younger and I fear somewhat excitable. I might have a word with Matthew Clarke. He is sure to keep an eye on the two of them," said Mary.

******

In the Gallagher home in Sunderland, Patrick dragged himself out of a warm bed taking his clothes from under the blankets. Shivering in the cold air, he climbed into his shirt and trousers. Having been sourly all morning, refusing to attend Mass with his wife and children, he left the chill of the bedroom to sit by the warm stove.

The young man mulled over his family's situation, things had been happening too fast for his liking. His eyes were drawn to the small window across the room and Patrick watched as a beam of dust-filled sunlight forced its way inside. It washed over an old kitchen table and highlighted the one splash of colour in his dismal surroundings – a single flower in a jar of water. Catherine's eyes lit up every time he brought one home to her and he never tired of her joyful reaction.

Two steps towards the window had Patrick warming his back in the sunlight as his eyes scanned the opposite wall. A deep crack ran jaggedly down its centre. If the family had still been living in the house behind, they could have passed cups of tea to each other, the opening was that wide in places. Catherine had stuffed the draughty gap with old newspapers in an attempt to keep the heat in their own house.

Patrick pulled open the door, allowing the warmth of a spring morning stream into the cottage. Breathing in a lungful of moist air, he stepped into the centre of the alley to survey the surrounding buildings. Of the sixteen houses that only a few years before had been home to more than eighty people, five were lived in. Each building had an identical one attached directly to its back. They would soon be demolished and Patrick's family forced to leave anyway. Giving in to Catherine's pleadings to return to Ireland had made sense at the time but the young man was beginning to regret that decision, as the move to Blackrock drew nearer.

The sound of his children's laughter could be heard before they even turned the corner into the alleyway and Patrick couldn't help but smile. Mary was carrying Maisie and young Tom launched himself into his father's arms.

"Mammy has a surprise for you. Close your eyes and hold out your hand," the little boy's eyes shone with delight.

Patrick complied and felt something small and light being placed on his palm.

"You can look now, Daddy."

"Is this all for me, Tom?" asked Patrick, licking his lips.

"It's only a wee cake," said Catherine. "We thought it might cheer you up."

"I think we can share it between us. Sure it's no fun eating such a delicacy on your own, is it?"

Patrick's doubts about moving melted away at the look of contentment on his wife's face. He hoisted Tom onto his shoulders and suggested they have their picnic in the park. Catherine protested that Maisie was too heavy for her to carry any further.

"Give her here to me," Patrick plucked his daughter from her mother's arms. "Don't I carry much more than the weight of these two every day at the quarry?"

"Aye, I suppose that's true. Sure if I get tired of walking a fine horse of a man like yourself would have no bother carrying the three of us home, would you?" teased Catherine

"No bother at all. In fact, I'd be carrying four of ye. You're forgetting about one of the children, aren't you?"

Catherine's hands automatically went to her swollen abdomen.

"Right so, it's off to the park with us. We might as well get used to being surrounded by grass, it won't be such a shock for the children when we move them to Ireland," laughed Patrick.

CHAPTER THREE

When Catherine saw her family standing on the quayside waving up at her she cried with joy. Even her aunt Maggie had turned up, sitting on the cart like Queen Victoria herself.

The young couple stepped off the boat carrying a child each. Breege took hold of Maisie while Mary snatched her grandson from his father's tight grip.

Hugs and kisses were exchanged while Patrick and James stood aloof, having shared a brief handshake.

"Look at her ladyship, sitting up there on her throne, like the Queen herself," Catherine gave a little curtsy to her aunt.

"Myself and the King here are quite happy in each other's company. Isn't that so, Rí?" Maggie called out to the donkey. "It took me so long to climb up here, I've no intention of repeating it for ye all to see and make fun of. Here, hand me up those poor wee mites before the life is squeezed out of them."

As Tom and Maisie were being lifted up to join their great-aunt, one of the ship's crew came over to Patrick and spoke to him. The young man nodded and pointed to the cart. James watched as the man walked away and wondered what his son-in-law was up to. Patrick could see him staring and skirted around the women, who were still embracing each other, tears of joy glistening on their cheeks.

"I brought something over from England but it's a wee bit heavy. Is it alright with you if we hoist it onto the cart?" Patrick inquired of James.

"I see you've already made the arrangement with one of the crew, so you might as well get on with it. As long as it doesn't do any damage, mind," was James's blunt reply.

Patrick cringed inwardly at the tone of his father-in-law's voice. He silently berated himself for not speaking to him first about using his cart to transport the surprise he had organized for Catherine.

"I'm sorry Maggie, you'll have to come down from your throne until we load something onto the cart. Here, let me help you," the young man held his arms up to her.

"You're a gentleman, Patrick, and no doubt about it," Maggie shot her brother a dagger of a look.

Putting her hands on the broad, muscular shoulders of the ex-quarryman, the older woman was taken aback at the change in him.

"I do declare, Patrick Gallagher, you've turned into a fine figure of a man," Maggie said, pinching his arms.

The young father's face coloured as he lifted his children down from the cart and handed them to Mary and Breege, before leading the donkey further along the quayside. He saw where the winch for lifting the cargo was positioned on the boat and placed the cart where one of the crew had directed. When Patrick looked back at his family he was amused by the confused look on their faces and beckoned to Catherine.

"What are you up to now?" she asked when she reached him.

Patrick stood her in front of him, facing the cart, and told her to close her eyes.

"On no account are you to open them, no matter what sounds you hear. I have a surprise for you," Patrick said as he steadied the donkey.

"What manner of a surprise is it that you have need of a cart?" Catherine looked back at her children and laughed. "I think your da has brought an elephant with him, all the way from England," she called out.

"Put your hands over your eyes, Catherine. No peeking, do you hear?" said Patrick.

Doing as she was told, the young wife felt foolish standing by the cart with her eyes shut tight and her family watching, along with a few other spectators. She heard the squeal of the pulleys as the ropes strained with the weight of their burden and then a soft thud amid the creaking of wood. The donkey tried to move forward as the cart took the load and the sound of his hooves stamping on the ground almost made Catherine open her eyes.

"You can look now," she heard Patrick say.

The sight of her old stove perched on top of the cart made her screech with delight as she threw herself into the young man's arms. Her heart swelled with joy at the love Patrick must have had for her, to go to all that trouble.

"You are the best husband any woman could wish for, Patrick Gallagher."

"Ah sure, I was only thinking of myself. Now you have no excuse not to make me a fine meal, have you?" Patrick teased.

CHAPTER FOUR

Catherine had just finished reading her brother's most recent letter from America, when her father stepped through the door. James saw the sheets of paper in her hand and smiled.

"I see your Aunt Maggie has you reading that rubbish about women voting. Thomas should know better than to encourage her with stories of such lunacy," he said.

"Stories of courage and determination you mean. What's her name? Susan is it?" asked Maggie.

"Susan B. Anthony. A name to be remembered, is that not so, Aunt Maggie?" responded Catherine.

The older woman smacked her hand off her knee and laughed.

"Our Thomas is a grand fella altogether," Maggie shook a finger at James. "The young men of today know where their loyalties should lie, and that woman Susan B. Anthony, deserves all the support she can get. Imagine having the nerve to cast a vote in an election knowing she was breaking the law, and then stand up in court as proud as punch about it. Mark my words, if women get the vote in America, it won't be long before we have it here."

"And who would you be voting for, if you could, Aunt Maggie?" asked Catherine.

"Oh, for heaven's sake, don't encourage her," said James. "I came over to give Patrick a message from the Murphy brothers. They're short of a man for their boat this evening, if he's interested. He should take the opportunity now, while there's a break in the weather. I can't go myself. Make sure he lets them know whether or not he'll be joining them. I'm off now, before my lunatic of a sister starts on another one of her rants."

As James left the house he could hear Maggie extolling the virtues of a local politician and he couldn't help but smile. His sister had become even more vocal as she got older and her talk of suffrage and equal rights for women did more to amuse the neighbours than influence them.

When Patrick arrived home, Catherine took great pleasure in telling him of the offer of a place on a boat for the evening. The smile that came to his face every time the opportunity of joining a crew came along assured her she had done the right thing in dragging him home to Ireland. Her young husband was a likeable man and offers of work regularly came his way whether it was labouring in the fields or other such casual employment.

People did not forget Patrick Gallagher once they had met him and his name would spring to mind whenever help was needed. Some of the jobs he was landed with made Patrick wish he hadn't been remembered so easily, however, being part of a crew on one of the Blackrock boats was not one of them.

"Will your da be going out, too? He usually fishes with the Murphy brothers, doesn't he?" asked Patrick.

"He can't go this evening. Be patient with him, love, this is his way of showing us he's beginning to accept you as family," said Catherine.

"He's just making sure his daughter and grandchildren are fed, that's what he's doing."

"Aye, you're not wrong, Patrick. My brother is as stubborn as an old goat, but you've been well and truly accepted by the rest of us, so don't fret over it, lad. He'll warm to you in time," said Maggie, "Is that not so, Ellen?"

Patrick smiled at the latest member of his young family, as she gurgled and wriggled at her belly being tickled.

"With the weather ruining most of the crops this year, there'll be little or no work in the harvesting. I'm thinking of going back to England for a while. I've three children to provide for now and milk won't satisfy our Ellen for much longer," said Patrick.

As Catherine put a platter of potatoes on the table she patted her husband's shoulder. She knew he was right about her father's reason for passing the job on to his son-in-law.

"Ah well, sure don't let it spoil the evening for you. Once you get out there in the bay, you'll forget all about my father and his sulking – and about going to England."

After their meal, Patrick sat his children on his lap and told them stories of old Irish myths. They especially loved his tales of the sea and young Tom would always ask his father to buy his own boat and take him out in it. Each time, Patrick would assure his son that he was saving every farthing for that very day and by the time he was finished school they would be fishing together.

Once Catherine had settled the children into bed, she joined Patrick and Maggie at the fireside. Sitting on his knee, she remarked on how calm the weather had been of late and hoped it didn't mean a storm was on the way.

"At the first sign of bad weather the boats will turn back. They always do, even when I, myself, wish they would stay a bit longer and take a chance. Maybe it's as well I don't have my own boat, you might find yourself widowed."

Catherine frowned and punched him in the shoulder.

"Patrick Gallagher, don't you dare tempt fate with that sort of talk. It's because you can swim that you're not afraid. There's nothing like the fear of drowning to make a man respect the sea and the weather."

CHAPTER FIVE

For once, it was Patrick who wanted to turn back to shore. The rest of the boats were already doing so, due to a squall that had suddenly come upon them, but a net full of fish was hard to leave behind. The Murphy brothers put it to a vote as to whether or not they should cut their losses and head for home.

Patrick had been the only one of the four men voting to leave the catch behind. While three of them struggled to haul in the net, the youngest crewman baled water out of the boat as fast as it was coming in. The heavy load dragged the vessel sideways in the swelling sea, while an ever increasing gale sent waves crashing over the men.

"We'll have to cut the net free and turn back, or we'll lose the boat," shouted Patrick above the screeching of the wind. "And our lives."

Waving his bone handled knife in the air, Patrick waited for a signal from one of the Murphys that would allow him to free the boat from a heavy weight threatening to drag them all to a watery grave. The older brother took out his own knife and shouted for Patrick to cut through the ropes. It wasn't long before their burden was released, sinking below the waves.

While Patrick helped the youngest member to bail water, the others rowed with all their might. As they drew closer to the shore the sea began to calm a little. Patrick had removed his boots earlier, tying them securely to the boat. He knew he would have a better chance of staying afloat without them, should he be washed overboard.

A crowd had gathered on the beach, watching and praying for the men to reach the shore and hopes were high that soon they would be on dry land. The men on the boat had begun to offer their own silent prayer of thanks when, out of nowhere, a monstrous wave reared up and flipped them over.

James McGrother and Matthew Clarke were already in a boat, preparing to set out for a rescue, should it be necessary. As soon as the giant swell struck, they began to row furiously in the direction of the upturned boat. The sea was choppy, but most of the wind had died down. James, who sat in the bow, glanced over his shoulder from time to time, trying to count how many heads were in the water. He could only see one person and they seemed to be hanging onto the upturned boat.

As they pulled up alongside the vessel the youngest member of the crew cried out for help and the two rescuers hauled him in beside them. While James questioned him about the other fishermen, his eyes scanned the sea around him. Matthew Clarke tied the upturned vessel to his own boat, as he too kept an eye out for the missing crew.

"Patrick pulled me up out of the water – *cough* – then he went down – *cough* – to look for the Murphy boys. He should be back up by now – *cough* –. Can either of ye see him?" the young man asked in between bouts of coughing up seawater from his lungs.

"Over there, James," Matthew Clarke shouted, grabbing hold of his oars.

"I see him, I see him," said James.

They rowed towards the exhausted young man who had just come up for air. Patrick had seen their approach but was frantically looking around him in the hopes of finding at least one of the Murphy brothers. Just as he was getting ready to dive once more, his father-in-law's voice rang out.

"Patrick Gallagher, think of your wife and children. The Murphys are gone. Get yourself into this boat and don't be foolish, man."

Ignoring the advice, Patrick disappeared below the surface and searched until he could no longer hold his breath. His ears began to ring and bright colours flashed before his eyes. As a feeling of serenity and calmness overtook him, Patrick slowly lost consciousness.

CHAPTER SIX

"Da, is it Patrick, tell me you have him in the boat. *DA?*"

The crowd waiting on the beach parted and hands began to pull Catherine through the gap, causing her to stumble.

"Let her through, it's his wife," someone shouted.

The words were like music to her ears at first, confirming that it was indeed Patrick, until the thought struck her that her young husband may not be alive. Was it his lifeless body that had been pulled from the sea?

As James and Matthew carried the unconscious fisherman towards a cart that was waiting by the roadside, Catherine grabbed Patrick's limp arm and shook it, crying out for him to wake up. Mary came running up from behind and took her daughter by the shoulders, holding her back.

"They're bringing him to Doctor Brunker's, Catherine. Leave him be, my love, every second counts."

"Oh, Ma. I don't think he was breathing. I didn't see his chest rise. I have to be with him."

"I know. I know. We'll follow them up to the doctor's house," Mary held Catherine out at arm's length. "Listen to me, now, girl. Did you take note of the vomit on his clothing? That means he coughed up what was in his lungs. Your da would have made sure of that as soon as he got him out of the water."

"Then why is he not awake, Ma?"

"It's the cold, Catherine. It does that to them if they've been in the water too long. Come on, he may very well be sitting up smiling when we get there, and wondering what all the fuss is about."

Mary didn't fully believe the words she had spoken but the look of hope they brought to her daughter's face was enough to calm her own anxious heart. The crowd had followed the cart, pulled by a young colt belonging to one of the gentry. A donkey would have travelled at a much slower pace and it was vital to get Patrick to the doctor's house as quickly as possible.

When Catherine and Mary arrived at the gate to Doctor Brunker's home, James was standing outside talking to one of their neighbours. He forced a smile at the two women as they approached and his heart went out to Catherine at the look of desperation across her young face.

"He's breathing more easily now that he's coughed up most of the sea water. Doctor Brunker has given him some sort of elixir that has made him bring up what was left in his lungs, so don't you go in there all fussing and fretting, do you hear me, girl?"

Catherine nodded and wiped tears from her cheeks. "Will I be allowed see him now, Da?"

"I'll go inside and see if he's finished bringing up his lungs first."

James disappeared and Mary led Catherine through the door to a chair in the hallway. Doctor Brunker came out from a room to the side of a wide, curving staircase and beckoned for the women to join him. He opened the door and smiled at Catherine. "He's a very fortunate young man. Another couple of minutes under water and he would have made you a young widow, my dear. Go on inside, your father is with him, but don't stay too long he needs his rest."

James stood up from the chair by the side of the bed as soon as the door opened. As his daughter rushed in and clung to her husband, he put an arm around Mary and steered her out of the room. Both parents breathed a sigh of relief once they were outside in the fresh air.

Alone with her husband, Catherine held one of his hands in a tight grasp, "Patrick, I thought I'd lost you. I told you not to tempt fate, didn't I? What happened out there?"

The young fisherman closed his eyes, resting his head back against a starched, white pillow. He was in a sitting position for ease of breathing and Catherine sat into the chair her father had vacated, to wait patiently for an answer to her question.

"I didn't want to stay out with the catch, but I'm not sure your da believes me. He is bound to think it was me who encouraged the Murphy boys to tarry behind when the others abandoned the fishing. After all, I was the oldest one on the boat, wasn't I?"

"Young Petey Halpin will tell them you didn't. He's hale and hearty and no worse off for the dunking he got, thanks to you by all accounts," said Catherine.

"And what of the Murphys? Is there any news of them? Will you go outside and ask, love? I cannot rest until I know."

The anguish written all over her husband's face was enough to convince Catherine that he spoke the truth. When she found Matthew Clarke it was with a heavy heart he gave her the sad news that the young men's bodies had been washed ashore. Their mother had been sedated by Doctor Brunker, with Maggie and a couple of the older women of the village offering to spend the night at the poor woman's house.

"She only has her two young daughters now, what will they do, with no men left in the family?" asked Catherine.

"What does any woman do, love? She'll get on with life as best she can. Her eldest girl works up at Freemont House now, so they will manage somehow," Mary said.

******

As the weeks went by and the village came to terms with the sad loss of two more fishermen, Patrick Gallagher found he was being viewed in a different light by all around him. Petey Halpin, the young man he had saved from drowning, never stopped singing his praises and recounted the story of what happened on that fateful day at every opportunity.

The attention Patrick received, although positive, caused him great discomfort. It wasn't the saving of one of the crew that filled his mind day and night but the loss of the other two men. Patrick replayed his actions over and over, trying to find a solution in his head that would give him peace.

'Should I have wasted precious minutes bringing young Halpin back to the boat? Petey might have reached it on his own, in spite of not being able to swim. Surely striking out in the water for the man furthest away would have been the right thing to do? Maybe at least one of

the Murphy boys would be alive today if I had done so.'

Two fine young men taken from an already fatherless family left a dark cloud hanging over Patrick. He began to call in on their mother each time he passed her house. She had been in her mid-thirties when she lost her husband to the sea and now found herself turning forty with her only sons suffering the same fate as their father.

Yet it was she who comforted Patrick.

"You cannot blame yourself for what happened. My boys should have turned the boat back when they saw the others heading for shore. They made a bad decision and paid the price for it."

"If any of the other men had the catch we had they might not have been so quick to give it up. I reckon they would have tried to bring it in, too. You can't blame your sons, Mrs. Murphy, for wanting to hold onto such a full net."

"I don't think badly of them for it, Patrick. They were young men, and as is often the case with youth, they were not so mindful of the danger."

A thought came into Patrick's head and while Mrs. Murphy continued speaking, it grew into a plan.

"What do you intend on doing with the boat? I suppose you'll be selling it," he asked.

"Well, I've no intention of bringing it out in the bay myself. No doubt, in time, I'll get offers."

"This might seem a foolish proposition to you, Mrs. Murphy, but would you consider holding onto the boat and letting me work it for you. I could give you the same portion of the catch as your family had before."

"Have you lost your senses, man? That would be three times what you yourself would get. You'd fare a lot better crewing another boat. Ah Patrick, it's good of you to think of us, but you have a family of your own to provide for," Mrs. Murphy was touched by such a generous offer.

"I'll be honest with you, I have wanted my own boat for a long time now. Would you consider a portion of the catch as payment towards the price of it?" asked Patrick.

"It would take you a mighty long time to purchase it that way. Think of how often the boats come in with a paltry catch, sure you'd be still buying it from my grandchildren at that rate," Mrs. Murphy shook her head. "I'm sorry Patrick, but if I get an offer I will have to accept it. The money will go a long way towards paying my rent."

"Ah sure, I suppose you're right. It was just a thought. I'd best be getting home now or Catherine will think I've left the country," said Patrick.

As he stood to leave, Mrs. Murphy held out her hand.

"I've changed my mind, Patrick. I would like to take you up on your offer of working our boat, if it still stands. At least until somebody shows an interest in purchasing it."

Patrick smiled as he shook the woman's hand, "You won't regret it, I promise you."

"Seeing as you won't be buying the boat from me, I think it only fair that we divide the catch equally between our families. Do we have an agreement?" asked Mrs. Murphy.

"Oh, we certainly do have an agreement, even if it only lasts for a week," Patrick was beaming.

Lamenting that many of the young men in the village where emigrating, leaving few to follow in the footsteps of their fishing kin, Mrs. Murphy felt it would be quite a while before any offers came in for the boat. The arrangement with Patrick Gallagher would mean she would still have fish to sell at market and feed to her family.

"There's not much money about these days, so I'm sure there'll be nobody beating down my door in their haste to purchase the boat."

It was an elated young man who made his way to his home at the other end of the village. Before he arrived at his door, Patrick had already made a list of the men he would ask to crew Mrs. Murphy's boat. His father-in-law was not one of them.

CHAPTER SEVEN

As Maggie drove the cart home after a good morning's sales at the market in Dundalk, she recounted an incident concerning her brother James when he was a child. Catherine marvelled at the ability of her aunt to remember so much from her youth.

"If my father knew the half of what you told me about him, he would be mortified, Aunt Maggie."

"Well now, I won't tell him if you don't," the older woman said, before going on to recount yet another story.

As the cart drew close to the post office in the village of Blackrock, a tall, dark haired man emerging from the building caught Catherine's eye. She gasped and pulled her shawl over her head, to hide her face.

"What's wrong with you, girl? It's a glorious day, you should be letting the fresh air into your lungs."

"I can feel a wee bite in the air. All those years in the doctor's house softened me, Aunt Maggie. I'm not as hardy as yourself."

Although tempted, Catherine was afraid to look behind her, for fear the man might recognize her, if he was the person she thought he was. She tried to convince herself that it was a mistake and felt sure that Blackrock was not the kind of place someone of his sort would travel to. Reprimanding herself for being so foolish, Catherine focused instead on yet another of her aunt's tales of the mischief her father had gotten up to as a young boy.

Later that evening, Catherine's younger brother arrived at her house, panting.

"Come in Jamie, and catch your breath. Is there trouble at home?"

The young boy shook his head vigorously before replying to his sister's question.

"No. No trouble. I raced over here to catch Patrick before he left for the boat," Jamie turned to face his brother-in-law. "I want you to take me out in the bay with you tonight."

There was an awkward silence and Catherine placed a hand on her brother's shoulder. She found it too difficult to say what was on her mind, but one look at her husband told her that he was thinking the same thing.

Jamie looked from one to the other of them and saw the closed expression on their faces. His mother had forbidden him to go out on a boat until he finished his schooling and no amount of begging on his part could ever change her mind.

"I'm past the age of twelve now and done with school. Ma always told me I could go when I was twelve. She knows I'm here."

"What did she have to say about it, Jamie?" asked Catherine.

The young boy told them how his mother was angry at first and had opened her mouth to give him her usual reprimand, whenever he broached the subject of being a fisherman.

"Then a strange look came over her face and she turned away saying, 'Go on, so. You're your father's son,' and I ran out the door before she could stop me," Jamie never took his eyes from Patrick as he spoke.

Knowing how her husband would respond, Catherine prayed he would let the boy down easily.

"I'm sorry, Jamie lad, but you'll have to bring me your father's permission, too. I cannot take you out tonight without it."

A big smile brightened the boy's face at Patrick's words and he jammed his cap onto his head as he turned on his heel to run into the street.

"Why did you get his hopes up like that?" asked Catherine. "You know my father will never let him crew your boat."

"It's not my boat, it belongs to Mrs. Murphy."

"I don't care who owns it. You should have said no to him as soon as he asked," Catherine replied sharply.

"What, and do his father's dirty work for him? If it were up to me, I'd have brought him along with us tonight. Let James McGrother watch the face of his own son crumple with disappointment when he withholds his permission."

Later that evening, as Patrick and Petey Halpin, along with two other men, brought their boat out into the bay alongside those who had left earlier, the low hum of men saying a rosary at midnight echoed across the still water. There were many superstitions the fishermen adhered to, some more than others, but the saying of the rosary was one that all the men took part in, even Patrick, who prided himself on being the least superstitious man in the village – and an atheist at that.

Just as the nets were being shot into the water, a boy's voice rang out, clear and strong.

33

"Patrick, over here? My da has me on his crew. Isn't it a -"

Jamie's sentence was cut short by a man's rebuke and there was a lot of muttering and laughter to be heard.

"Sorry, I meant to say Mr. Clarke's crew," the young voice shouted out.

Patrick Gallagher exchanged smiles with the men on his boat and waved back at the silhouette of young Jamie McGrother, his twelve year old frame a dark shape against the star studded midnight sky. One of his father-in-law's endearing qualities, was that he couldn't bear to disappoint anyone, if it was within his power to avoid it. *The only exception he makes is in his dealings with me,*' thought Patrick. *'He would happily spend the rest of his life making me miserable, given half a chance.'*

CHAPTER EIGHT

When Catherine returned from selling Patrick's share of the previous night's catch she was happy to find her two eldest children curled up asleep each side of their father, having an afternoon nap. They had been listening to one of his stories and all three of them had fallen asleep.

Handing over baby Ellen to Maggie, who was sitting by the fire having put some bread in a crock to bake, the young woman poured them both some tea.

"How are the Murphy girls doing, Catherine? It's been two months since they lost their brothers, bless them. And their poor mother, how was she this morning? Did she go to town with you?"

"She did, Maggie. Sure it gives her a break from the house and its memories, sharing the journey to market with me. Did you know she got rid of every stitch of her sons' clothing? Her youngest girl was sleeping with them under her mattress, crying all night long."

Maggie nodded in the direction of Patrick and his two little ones snuggled into him, "Sure look at your wee ones beside their father, all safe and sound. There's no feeling like it, is there? That wee Murphy girl was very attached to her two brothers, I suppose they took the place of her father, rest his soul. Now she's lost them, too. A terrible tragedy. Terrible."

Wanting to change the subject, Catherine asked her aunt if she had noticed anything different about her sister Mary-Anne.

"Now you mention it, I have. She's not as sour as usual. I caught her smiling two days in a row. Do you think she has a man?" asked Maggie.

"Ah, she's not that bad. Mary-Anne had it hard as a child, always sickly, missing out on school and playing with other children. She's been a lot better since coming back to Ireland."

"You're too forgiving, Catherine," tutted Maggie. "That girl is always trying to cause trouble between you and Patrick. And she stirs up her father no end when the men are in each other's company."

Catherine laughed, "Aye, Mary-Anne knows how to raise Da's hackles when he's around Patrick, I'll agree with you there. But I never let what she says come between myself and my man. She's not good with words, Aunt Maggie. Sometimes what comes out of her mouth isn't what she intended."

"Ah would you stop defending her, Catherine. I'm telling you now, watch your back where your sister, Mary-Anne, is concerned."

Her aunt's words played on Catherine's mind as the day wore on and while Patrick left the house later in the afternoon, to help a neighbour with a bit of work, she decided to pay a visit to her mother. Knowing that Mary-Anne and Breege would be working at the Blackrock Hotel in the village, Catherine knew there would be an opportunity to speak to her mother in private.

When she arrived at her parents' home, James was sitting on a chair by the fire reading a letter. When he looked up to greet her, she could tell it wasn't good news.

"Has Thomas written at last?"

"He has, did your mother tell you?" asked James.

"I haven't seen her today, is she around?"

"She has gone to the graveyard."

Catherine knew that meant only one thing. Mary had taken to visiting Pat and Annie's grave whenever something bothered her.

"Is it bad news from America, so?" asked Catherine.

James nodded and handed the letter to his daughter, "But our Thomas thinks it's the best thing that has happened to him in a long time," he said.

While her father poured out two cups of tea, Catherine read the neat script, skimming across the news of any neighbours her brother had bumped into. When she came to the part where Thomas announced his plans to get married again, she looked up at her father.

"He never spoke of a woman in any of his other letters. Did you know he was courting, Da?"

James shook his head, "This is the first I've heard of it. Do you see now why your Ma is upset?"

"But sure he's widowed," Catherine read a woman's name aloud from the letter, "Lily McCann. She sounds as if she's Irish. I hope she's good to him. Thomas doesn't say much about her, that's not like him."

"No, he doesn't, but that's not what has your ma upset. She's grown very fond of wee Eliza, sure we all have."

No sooner were the words out of her father's mouth than Catherine raced out the door crying, "Poor Ma."

Mary was sitting on the ground at Pat and Annie's grave, her face cradled in her hands. Catherine knew her mother was not praying, but weeping. She hesitated before joining her, knowing she was intruding on a very private moment.

"I've just read Thomas's letter, Ma. I know what's upsetting you. He would never take Eliza away from you, she's been with ye these past seven years. Sure, she's only been in his company four or five times since he left. I'll write and remind him of how well she's doing here and how happy she is," Catherine tried to console her mother.

"Do you think he's upset that she calls me her ma?" asked Mary.

"Of course he's not. Isn't it grand for her to feel that way? Especially when her father is so far away and she hardly ever sees him. Sure don't we all make sure Eliza grows up knowing Thomas is her father?

Mary seemed to brighten up a little at Catherine's words, "Do you remember Thomas's last visit and the look on his face when she dragged your da across the room to him, saying, *'Come on, Dadó, shake hands with Da.'* Your poor brother, I thought he was going to burst into tears," said Mary.

"Aye, it truly touched his heart to hear his wee one call him *Da*. There wasn't a dry eye in the house that day," replied Catherine.

For a long time, mother and daughter sat together on the damp grass, breaking the silence between them now and again with the sharing of a cherished memory. Catherine thought she saw extra wisps of grey in her mother's hair and noticed how unusually pale she was that day.

"Ma, are you not feeling well? Or is it the sadness has you looking as white as a sheet?"

Mary patted her daughter's hand before leaning on her shoulder to stand up.

"I'm getting old, that's all, my love. Getting old and maudlin. Ask your father, he's half afraid to talk to me lately, for fear I might start weeping and wailing."

"Ma, you're not yet fifty. Don't be talking nonsense."

"It's true, Catherine. I want you to promise me that you'll look after your father, should I pass on before him."

"I'll do no such thing. I refuse to even think about it. But I *will* take you to a doctor. You must be ailing to be thinking like that."

Mary could see the concern written all over Catherine's face, "We'll see. I will do as you ask if there's no improvement in me by the end of the week. Does that ease your mind somewhat?"

Catherine was happy with her mother's response and the two women made their way home, arm in arm, both of them in much better frames of mind.

******

In Paddy Mac's the talk was all about politics. The men had been discussing the 1874 elections held earlier that year.

"It's a far cry from the day when men were marched into town and forced to cast their vote openly in front of their landlords," someone commented.

"Aye, the secret ballot has put an end to that, at least."

"With fifty-nine seats won by members of the Home Rule League, it won't be long till Ireland has control of her own destiny," said Paddy Mac.

"I wouldn't be holding my breath for that," said Matthew Clarke. "The League's members don't even belong to the same political parties. Isaac Butt himself is Conservative and sure the only reason they won is because of seats not being contested."

"Never mind the politics, men. What about the weather we've been having, taking its toll on the harvest it is. Even my wee bit of a garden is suffering," an elderly man piped up.

James was glad of a change of topic, adding to the conversation about the weather. "If these storms continue, we'll have neither fish nor fodder, then we'll be in a right mess. With nothing to harvest and no boats going out, it'll be over to England again for most of us."

As mutterings of agreement rippled through Paddy Mac's cosy establishment, its turf fire throwing out a welcome heat, the storm outside seemed to echo James's statement. The wind driven rain lashed against the window panes and the men gave each other knowing glances as they were reminded that no matter who was governing them, they would always be at the mercy of the weather.

CHAPTER NINE

Taking in the fresh sea air on one of the few calm days that autumn, Catherine and Mary-Anne walked alongside the sea wall that separated the beach from the road. Everyone had the same idea and the whole village seemed to be either sitting on the wall, standing in doorways chatting to neighbours or walking at a leisurely pace, like the two sisters.

"You've been very happy in yourself lately, Mary-Anne. It's good to see you so cheerful. You have a lovely smile, you know," said Catherine.

"And what exactly does that mean?" asked Mary-Anne, ignoring the compliment and pulling away from her sister.

The young women had been linking arms but now they stood facing each other, one with a look of confusion on her face the other wearing a hostile scowl.

"I didn't mean to offend you. I'm not the only one to have noticed the change in you. Well, I won't beat around the bush. Do you have a suitor? As your older sister I have your best interest at heart, Mary-Anne."

"Oh you have, is that so? And did you have my best interest at heart when you stole the one man I cared about, right out from under my nose?"

Catherine was astounded at her sister's accusation. It was the first time Mary-Anne had given voice to her real feelings about Patrick. There had always been hints and undertones but never an outright admission.

"I'm sorry you feel that way, but Patrick has never felt anything for you other than a brotherly affection. It wasn't until we moved back home that I realized how you felt about him," Catherine knew she should be angry at her sister but all she could feel was sympathy.

"I suppose it was our dear Aunt Maggie that informed you of that little piece of gossip. Well, I wouldn't be so sure of your husband's devotion, if I were you. I've seen the way he looks at me behind your back. It wouldn't take much to lure him away from you, Catherine. You should be thankful that I care about you too much to cause you such pain."

As Mary-Anne linked her arm, Catherine was shocked and at a loss for words. She was so absorbed in her thoughts that she almost bumped into a tall dark haired man, standing directly in front of them.

"Good afternoon, ladies."

The voice froze Catherine to the spot as her eyes moved up slowly from the highly polished leather shoes to a face that once haunted her dreams. Her shoulder jerked slightly as Mary-Anne, still linking her arm, gave a tiny curtsy and giggled.

"Why Doctor Gilmore, is your good wife taking one of her afternoon naps on such a lovely day as this?"

"She is indeed, Mary-Anne. Such a waste of a nice break in the weather, don't you think? And who is this vision beside you? She must surely be your sister, for you both share the same exquisite beauty." Gilmore bowed, his hat in hand.

"This is my sister, Catherine. She's married and those are her two over there," said Mary-Anne. "Tom, come over here and bring your sister with you," she called out to her nephew.

Catherine was beginning to recover her composure as the old feelings of hatred and disgust came back to her.

"Say hello to Doctor Gilmore, Tom, and introduce him to your sister. Catherine has three children altogether, a right old married lady she is now. Aren't you, my dear?" Mary-Anne's face was flushed with excitement.

Gilmore knelt down on one knee and drew Tom close. His eyes almost devoured him and the scene caused an icy fear to smother any feelings of hatred Catherine was harbouring.

"Pleased to meet you, sir," said Tom. "This is my sister, Maisie. Our baby sister is at home with Aunt Maggie. Her name is Ellen."

"Come away from the gentleman now, Tom, and let him get on with his walk. Good day to you," Catherine pulled her children back from Gilmore.

The doctor, still on one knee, took a coin from his pocket and held it out.

"Buy something nice for yourself and your sister, Tom," he said.

Even Catherine heard the softness in his voice as he spoke but it didn't change her feelings toward him. She pulled her son's outstretched hand back, before the coin could be placed on his small palm.

Mary-Anne was shocked at her sister's rudeness and reached out to take the proffered money.

"Please forgive Catherine's bad manners, Doctor Gilmore. I shall be happy to accept your coin on behalf of the children and see to it that they have a nice treat."

Gilmore smiled charmingly at the young woman as he placed the money in her hand, slowly curling her fingers around it, causing Mary-Anne to blush. The attention from such a well-mannered gentleman was more than she could ever have hoped for – and in public at that.

Catherine grabbed hold of Tom's hand and lifted Maisie onto her hip as she turned from a scene that brought bile to the back of her throat. Tears of frustration and anger stung at her eyes and she dragged her protesting son along the street, putting as much distance as possible between him and the man who almost ruined her life. Vaguely aware of the strange looks she was getting from the people she passed by, Catherine struggled to contain her emotions.

'Why would he do such a thing?' she thought. *'Making a fool of a young woman like that. Is it by coincidence that he has come here, or is he intent on making trouble for me? I will just have to make sure I stay well out of his way. If he thinks he can take my son, he can think again. I would die first rather than let that happen.'*

"Catherine, CATHERINE," Patrick's voice cut into her frantic thoughts. "You're frightening the children. What has you in such a panic?" he had pulled Maisie out of her arms.

The look of confusion on her son's face as he clung to his father's trouser leg brought Catherine to her senses. How was she to explain

44

her behaviour without revealing a terrible secret that she feared would destroy her marriage? It was Patrick who unknowingly provided her with an answer.

"Did Mary-Anne say something to upset you?" he asked.

Catherine looked back down the street and saw her sister walking slowly towards them, greeting people as she passed them by.

"She did, Patrick. She said something so hurtful it made me feel ill. Can we please go back to the house now, before she reaches us and we have a disagreement right here on the street, in front of half the village?"

Patrick could see how distressed his wife was and without needing any further explanation, he quickly turned and led his family away from Mary-Anne, who was beginning to pick up her pace.

Maggie was sitting on a chair outside the open door as they approached and for once didn't notice that anything was wrong as they entered the house. She had her eyes closed and her face up to the sun.

"That heat is doing a world of good to my old bones. Come back outside here and make the most of it while it lasts," she shouted.

Tom and Maisie came running out to her and began to play at her feet with some shells they had put into their pockets on the beach. Raised voices reached their ears from within the cottage and Maggie stood to close the door. As she did so, she was surprised to see Catherine in tears while Patrick paced back and forth in front of her.

"Why are they not happy on such a lovely day, Aunt Maggie?" asked Tom.

"Grownups are no different to children when it comes to feeling sad or happy. The weather can make them feel both, but the things people do or say can be even more powerful than the weather."

"It wasn't Da who made her cry. It was Mary-Anne and that strange man we met."

"What man? Was he a friend of Mary-Anne's?" Maggie's curiosity was heightened.

"She knew his name. She called him Doctor something. He tried to give me a coin but Ma wouldn't let me take it. Mary-Anne told her she was being rude and took the money for us. Do you think she'll keep it, Aunt Maggie? I hope she lets us buy some sweets. What kind would you like, Maisie?"

Maggie had heard enough. It was obvious to her that Mary-Anne had once again tried to come between the young couple and this time she had been very successful. The mystery doctor was somehow involved in all of this and Maggie wondered if he was the reason behind the change in Mary-Anne.

The door being wrenched open jolted Maggie out of her thoughts and Patrick stormed past her, shouting back that he would be readying the nets for the night's fishing. It had been a week since anyone had brought a boat out, the weather being so bad of late. Maggie told the children to remain outside in the evening sunshine, reminding Tom that he was the eldest and should watch over his little sister.

"Catherine, what ails you, my love? Patrick had a look of thunder on his face as he left. I'll make us some tea."

"It was a bit of a quarrel with Mary-Anne that got me upset, Aunt Maggie. I was foolish to listen to her, sure you know what she's like."

"Aye, so Tom says. Who was the doctor ye were talking to? The one that offered a coin to him."

Maggie watched her niece's face closely as she answered the question.

Taking a sip of tea while considering just how much her aunt should be told, Catherine realized that she had no one to confide in. Rose was far away and not very good at reading, so she couldn't even write to her about what had happened. She desperately needed advice from someone who could think clearly, but Maggie was not the one to turn to.

"I think he is the reason why our Mary-Anne has been so pleasant lately. He's very charming and she seems to be letting his flattery go to her head. I fear that his motives are not good and he will lead her astray."

"And you said as much to Mary-Anne, is that so?"

Catherine nodded her head and continued to sip her tea.

"Your sister is very jealous of you, have you not realized that, yet?" asked Maggie.

"I do now. She said I stole Patrick out from under her nose and that he gives her looks behind my back that tell her she means more to him than I do. I know it's not true but it riled me to hear her say it."

"Patrick was never anywhere near your sister's nose. He has always considered her a nuisance. It's only because your mother is so protective of her that he never complains openly. Mary-Anne believes whatever she wants to and there's no changing her mind when it's made up."

Maggie put some food into Catherine's hands and told her to go to her husband with it, as he had not eaten anything that afternoon. Offering to feed the children and put them to bed, Maggie assured her niece that by the time Patrick had walked to the boats he would have shaken off the temper he was in.

Grateful for the opportunity to go after her husband, Catherine walked hastily through the village, praying she would not bump into either Gilmore or her sister. As it was still early evening, Patrick was alone as he tended the nets. He didn't see his wife's approach and jumped with fright when she said his name close behind him.

"If I were a cat and you a mouse you'd be in my belly by now," Catherine gave a nervous laugh.

"You shouldn't sneak up on people like that, you could get eaten yourself. I'm sorry I left the house in such a temper. I've walked it off, so you can rest easy. If the sea takes me tonight our last words to each other will have been pleasant ones."

"That's not why I followed you, Patrick. I know you would never take a boat out with a clouded mind. Especially with such a young crew on board. I wanted to apologize for my behaviour in the street, I should know better

48

than to let Mary-Anne's silly talk upset me like that."

Patrick put the nets down and turned to look directly at his wife. Even though her voice had sounded light, her face betrayed the way her heart was feeling.

"It's your sister who should be apologizing, not you, Catherine. I'm frustrated that I am not permitted to defend you when she hurts you with her vicious tongue."

"Patrick, you know that it would break Ma's heart if she were to find out the things that Mary-Anne has said to me. The only way I can put up with it is to forgive her. Can you not do that, too? For the sake of peace."

"I cannot forgive her, but I will suffer it as long as you can, love. When it becomes too much for you, then I *will* act. I thought you may have had your fill of it this evening, when I saw how upset you were."

As Catherine threw herself into his arms, thanking him for his patience, Patrick saw the rest of his crew approach behind her. There were hoots and whistles from the young men, causing Catherine to pull out of her husband's arms, a flush of embarrassment colouring her cheeks.

"I tripped," she muttered as she hurried past them. "Mind yourselves tonight and don't be taking the calm weather for granted. I'll see you in the morning, Patrick," she shouted back.

CHAPTER TEN

Every time Catherine tried to change the subject her mother brought it right back to the same thing. It was difficult for Mary to keep bottled up the pride she felt at Mary-Anne's accomplishments. The bread and cakes she baked for the hotel were in huge demand by the clientele. They loved to have her wait on their tables and gave her gifts and money at the end of their stay.

"How your sister has blossomed since she took up that position in the hotel. Nobody would believe she was the same girl who had been emptying chamber pots and changing bedsheets for years before that. Why, she is almost as sweet as you, love."

"Yes, Ma. I can see the change in her, outwardly at least."

"Why Catherine McGrother, please do not tell me that it's you who is jealous of Mary-Anne now. That would be a turnaround, no doubt about it," Mary smiled and patted her daughter's hand.

"My name is Gallagher, Ma, not McGrother. And that is why I could never be jealous of my sister, no matter how wonderful her life appears to be."

"Did she tell you about her latest good fortune?" Mary carried on. "One of the guests has asked her to be a companion for his wife while he returns to England. He's a doctor, no less, and will pay Mary-Anne for her services. His poor wife is ailing and the air here suits her well."

A tight knot was forming in Catherine's stomach and she placed her cup on the table with shaking hands.

"I'm sorry, Ma. I must be going. I have a lot of chores to do."

She kissed her mother on the cheek before taking her leave and had to bite her tongue at the words that were spoken softly in her ear.

"Don't be letting envy take a hold of you, my love. It's not in your nature."

It was a very quiet and pensive young woman who dished up supper for her family in the Gallagher home later that evening. Patrick waited until the children were asleep before tackling his wife about her mood. He asked if he had done something to offend her and accepted her assurance that there was nothing about him that was causing her any trouble.

"Did your sister tell you about her good fortune?"

"Which sister, Patrick?"

"Mary-Anne. She was boasting about her new position as a lady's companion. Maybe she'll leave us alone now and we'll have some peace," said Patrick.

"Ma told me. Can I ask you a question about my sister?"

"Which sister?" Patrick smiled.

"The one who complained to me about a month ago that you were following her wherever she went."

Patrick laughed and asked Catherine if she truly believed such nonsense.

"Then why do you tell me you're going to tend the nets and when I pass by the boat, you are nowhere to be seen?"

The young husband laughed even louder and Catherine shushed him with a warning not to wake their children.

"If I tell you where I was you must promise not to breathe a word to anyone."

"Patrick just tell me the truth. Where you meeting up with Mary-Anne or not?" irritation was getting the better of Catherine.

"I was teaching Petey Halpin to swim. He didn't want me to tell anyone, that's why I never said where I was going.

Patrick drew a very embarrassed Catherine onto his lap and loosened her hair from its bun. As the long wavy tresses fell onto her shoulders, he kissed her cheek and tasted the salt of a tear.

"I have no interest in Mary-Anne. Why would I, with such a beauty as yourself by my side? You should have asked me sooner, love, if it bothered you so much. You are like your father in that respect, brooding over something instead of speaking your mind."

Catherine stood up and walked slowly towards the bed in the corner of the parlour, which made Patrick think he may have hurt her feelings.

Maggie had retired earlier with the children, to the small room that had been built onto the back of the cottage when Kitty Carroll lived there. The quietness of the house seemed more obvious to Patrick as he watched his wife braid her hair, as she sat on the edge of their bed. She kept her eyes averted from his gaze, but was acutely aware of him looking at her. As she pulled together the heavy curtains surrounding their bed, Catherine raised her eyes and smiled at Patrick.

"I might be like my father but I love you a wee bit more than he does."

It wasn't long before the young couple were wrapped in each other's arms, discarding any feelings of doubt or anxiety. Unfortunately, Catherine was soon to find out that it wasn't Mary-Anne's jealousy she should be concerned about, but something much more threatening to their relationship.

CHAPTER ELEVEN

The air of excitement that permeated the room was enough to make even the most pessimistic man there hopeful. A large group of men had turned up to hear what the visiting speaker had to say. As words such as equality and cooperation rang out, the old familiar desire for justice stirred in Patrick's heart.

The International Working Men's Association had recently formed branches in Belfast, Cork, Dublin and Cootehill and it was from the latter town that three men had arrived to rally support from local people.

As Patrick walked home to a wife who thought he was having a drink in Paddy Mac's, his mind was filled with the hope of a better life for his young family. It made no difference to him what kind of an accent a man spoke with, his own being a mix of Irish and English. Changing the flag of a country didn't necessarily mean better conditions for the majority of its people and Patrick truly believed that a much more radical approach was needed.

So as not to make a liar out of himself, Patrick dropped into Paddy Mac's and was surprised at how few men were there.

"I'm glad I called in to give you a bit of business, Paddy. You don't appear to be earning too much this evening."

"Ah, it's the weather has everyone cowering indoors. That and the fact that there's no money to be earned around these parts lately. But I don't worry about it too much, Patrick, for the men cannot bear to be cooped up in the house for too long," Paddy Mac poured the young man his usual beverage. "Another day of this weather and we'll be packed so tight, I won't have need of a fire to warm the place. The only ones to show their faces this evening are the likes of yourself, only living a stone's throw away."

Patrick took a mouthful of the drink set before him, then placed himself in front of the blazing fire. As a cloud of steam rose from his soaking clothes, Paddy Mac commented that he must have walked at a snail's pace to arrive so wet.

"I was on my way back from town when the heavens opened. I felt like I was in the middle of a waterfall, the rain was that heavy. It's after easing off a bit now. I'll go home as soon as I've finished my drink, in case it starts up again."

The adrenalin from the meeting he had attended earlier had not been completely dissipated by his two mile journey on foot, and Patrick could not hold back from sharing with Paddy Mac the words that had made such a big impression on him.

"Well, what do you think yourself? Do you not see why the whole country should be supporting this, Paddy?"

"I haven't come across that crowd before, they must be very new, alright. But there's not many here would be interested in going to Cootehill, Patrick. Not by my reckoning anyways. It's the likes of those poor unfortunates in the factories that will take the trouble. What business does a village full of fishermen have with a rally such as that?"

"Because we are all labourers, whatever manner of work we do. We should be paid a fair wage for a fair day's work. Women, too, they are exploited even more so than men. And children are the most vulnerable of all," Patrick was repeating the words that had captivated him earlier.

"But sure it's always been that way. Isn't that what class and money shields you from, a life of hard work and little means," one of Patrick's neighbours had joined the conversation.

"Hard work isn't such a bad thing, if it's justly rewarded," said Patrick. "When the herrings are in the bay do we not all work harder than ever because of the season? And harvesting a crop, we do the same."

"And when there's not a fish to be caught or a crop to be brought in due to bad weather, who pays us then? When there's no work to be had," another man asked.

"If we were better paid we would have enough savings to cover hard times. Maybe then we could afford the rent increases laid upon us when the landlords suffer a loss of revenue from their crops," Patrick replied.

He looked around Paddy Mac's and realized that he was the youngest man there. The tanned, weather-lined faces looking back at him belonged to men old enough to be his uncles, if he had any left. With a sigh, Patrick admitted to himself that he would be wasting his time trying to rouse support in a fishing village. Most of the younger men had either emigrated or taken up seasonal work in England.

Draining the last drop of his ale, Patrick wiped a line of froth from his moustache and bade goodnight to the room.

"I suppose this is not the place for such talk. It will be in the big towns and cities that the change will come about. I'm off to my bed, with any luck there'll be a day's work to be had tomorrow. I've a nest of hungry mouths at home to feed."

As Patrick turned to leave, one of the men called out to him.

"It's not that we don't agree with what you say, son, but it will be up to the likes of yourself, young and full of spirit, to bring about the change. Don't lose heart, Patrick."

Those words rang in the young man's ears as he ran home with the wind beating the rain into his face. He pulled his cap low onto his forehead, which offered a small amount of protection to his eyes but when he finally reached his door Patrick's face had been scrunched up so much, the muscles ached when he tried to relax them.

"We could do with a decent break in the weather, love. There's no one foolish enough to bring a boat out in that, not even me."

Catherine watched in silence as her husband peeled off his wet clothes. She had banked the fire and was sitting mending a tear in one of her aunt's aprons. It belonged to the hotel where Maggie had been working as a cleaner since her return from England.

While Patrick was turned away from her, Catherine let her eyes linger on his broad back and slender waist. She had always loved his shoulders and how they formed a wide triangle with the rest of his upper torso. Her stomach lurched at the thought of another woman gazing with the same longing at the man standing before her. The feeling intensified as Mary-Anne's taunting came to mind.

Swinging around as he draped a blanket across his shoulders, Patrick caught the look on her face and mistook it for worry over their lack of funds.

"Don't worry, Catherine love, I've a feeling I'll get some work tomorrow and as soon as the weather eases up we'll have the boats back out again." Patrick pulled his chair closer to the heat of the fire.

"Did you spend the entire evening in Paddy Mac's? You don't smell as if you did."

Patrick was taken aback at the sharpness in his wife's tone.

"Would you rather I drank more and let my children go hungry?" he shot back.

Aware that a row was brewing, the young husband announced that he was tired and turned towards his bed, but was stopped in his tracks by the words he next heard.

"My father called here earlier this evening with word of a job for you tomorrow. So your feeling was right, wasn't it? A pity you weren't in Paddy Mac's or he could have put your mind at ease about feeding your children."

As he bit his lower lip, Patrick tried to think up a reasonable excuse for not being found by his father-in-law.

"He must have been there when I was out walking. Sure I couldn't sit in Paddy Mac's all night with one drink in front of me now, could I?" said Patrick.

"Aren't you the fool to go out walking in such weather and you having suffered from such a bad bout of *pneumonia* when you first arrived here," Catherine said, sarcastically.

"You know well I've never suffered from that. It doesn't suit you to be so sharp. Do I have to answer to where I spend every minute of my day? Your father could have left a message at Paddy Mac's if he had a mind to."

"He was sure you'd be here in such weather so he came straight over. Got soaked to the skin doing so. He said for you to call to the house before the children go to school and he'll tell you about the work," Catherine put her sewing away and stood up, taking a deep breath.

"When I asked after Ma and the family, Da said they were all fine but that he hadn't seen Mary-Anne since yesterday, as she was spending a few days with Mrs. Gilmore at the hotel. Was it as far as there you walked in such bad weather, Patrick?"

Before he could answer, Catherine rushed past him and dived onto their bed, unable to control her anger any longer. Patrick knew if he owned up to attending the meeting earlier that evening, it would only make matters worse and give her more to worry about. He sat for an hour by the fire, shivering in his blanket until he was sure Catherine had fallen asleep.

As he pulled the cover from his shoulders to drape across his fully clothed wife, asleep on the edge of the bed, Patrick prayed that his movements would not disturb her. He eased himself under the covers, still shaking with the chill in his bones and thought how ironic it would be, if he was to fall victim to pneumonia

59

as a punishment for not being honest with his wife.

CHAPTER TWELVE

Having just completed his last assignment for his editor, Thomas made his way home through the slums of New York. Women in doorways called out to him suggestively, some extremely young, made up to look older. Barefoot children chasing swine through the dung filled alleyways brought to mind his own daughter back in Ireland. Thomas missed her sorely and tried to remember the feel of her soft arms against his neck, her hands folded under his chin as he gave her piggy-backs around his mother's garden.

Lily was folding clothes and stacking them in a neat pile when he arrived at their tiny bedsit.

"I was paid well for that last assignment, so we can rest easy while we are in Ireland," said Thomas.

"I was under the impression you had to work while we were there. Does that mean we can spend more time together?" Lily kissed an unshaved cheek, "I hope you're going to get rid of those bristles before we leave. I want a respectable looking man on my arm when I board the ship, even if we must travel steerage."

Thomas swept Lily into his arms and scrubbed her neck with his chin. As she pushed him away they both tripped and landed on the bed, on top of the pile of neatly folded clothes.

"Sorry, my love, but we don't have time for any canoodling," said Lily. "Help me up before I succumb to your charms."

While Lily refolded the clothes, Thomas explained for the tenth time how important it was that his family think they had married in a church. A civil ceremony was not something his parents would be happy to hear about.

"So who was it married us?"

"Father McEvoy," replied Lily, holding up a pair of white gloves.

"And what church and parish was it?"

"Saint Raymond's of Castle Hill," she sighed.

Lily gave Thomas a sly grin, "And we spent three days and nights in bed in a fancy hotel with our food left on trays outside the door of our room."

"That's the only part of our story that's true, but you can't mention it, especially not to Ma. I'd never be able to face her again."

"For a journalist, you are certainly very prudish, Thomas. This is the nineteenth century, after all. Most adults are well aware of what goes on between newly-weds."

"Not in Ireland. Or if they are, nobody talks about it, at least not the way you do. That would be considered men's talk," Thomas thought for a moment. "Except for my aunt Maggie. You'll get along just fine with her."

"So you are always telling me. I cannot wait to meet this woman that I remind you so much of. There, all packed. I think I did very well, forcing so much into such a small trunk, even if I do say so myself."

******

Noticing the strain between her two eldest girls, Mary tried to ease the tension by reminding them of the anticipated arrival of their brother and his new wife. It seemed to work and Mary-Anne remarked on the fact that they would be staying in the hotel where she worked.

"It will seem strange not having Thomas here with us, but then I suppose his wife would like to have a little privacy, her being a city person and all," said Mary.

"We offered them a place to stay too, Ma, but Thomas said they would prefer not to be a burden on anyone," Catherine added.

"If he was travelling alone he would not think twice about burdening us with his presence. I hope his new wife is truly as pleasant as he describes in his letters," said Mary-Anne. "I would hate to think of our dear Thomas being married to a snob."

Mary and Catherine exchanged discreet smiles, for everyone knew that the young woman, who had recently become a companion to one of the hotel guests, was quite a snob herself.

"Now, Mary-Anne, don't be judging the poor girl before you've even met her. She's your sister-in-law, after all. We must give her a warm welcome and see to it that she is made to feel at home."

"I'm not judging her, Ma, but I find it hard to understand why Thomas would prefer a hotel room to a bed in his parents' home. It's not like him at all, especially with him being one of them *radicals* or whatever it is he calls himself nowadays."

"Hush your mouth, Mary-Anne. If you knew what it was like to be a newly-wed, you would understand why they need their privacy," hissed Catherine.

Mary stood up and placed herself between the two sisters, blocking their view of each other. She had never before heard her eldest daughter speak with such venom in her voice.

"Well some of us have work to do. I had better start my bread-making before the morning is completely gone. Your father will be home for a bite to eat at midday. Is Patrick out for the day, Catherine? Must you be getting back to prepare a meal yourself?"

Her mother's words brought Catherine to her senses and the anger she felt towards her sister left as quickly as it had flared up. Thankful that she had been given the perfect excuse to take her leave, she kissed her mother's cheek.

"Oh my goodness Ma, I wasn't aware of the time slipping by, I had best be getting back."

Patrick had no intention of arriving home until later that evening, and Catherine was well aware of the fact. An uneasiness lay between them, and neither one was willing nor able to bridge the gap that had been slowly pushing them apart. None of this escaped Maggie's notice but for once she was lost for any words that might help the young couple.

Later that day, walking back towards her home after a busy day at the hotel, Maggie spied Patrick talking to Petey Halpin and suddenly developed a limp as she drew near them.

"Oh Patrick, son. What a sight for sore eyes you are – or sore legs, if I'm to be truthful."

"Why are you limping, Maggie? Have you had a fall?" asked Patrick, taking hold of her arm.

"I'm getting old, that's what ails me. Are ye finished your talking, by any chance? Only I could do with a good strong man like yourself to lean on, or I might still be trying to get home this time tomorrow."

The men laughed and Petey bade them farewell as Maggie linked her arm through Patrick's for the rest of the walk home.

"If I tell you a secret, you must promise not to breathe a whisper of it to anyone. Do I have your word on it, Patrick?"

"You can keep your old secrets to yourself, Maggie. I don't need the burden of them, if you don't mind."

"Ah, Patrick. I'm fit to burst with this one. I have to tell someone or I might let it out to the others," Maggie took a deep breath and didn't wait for a response from her companion. "Thomas and his fine young wife are here already. I was talking to them at the hotel. So was Mary-Anne. They're staying there, you know. Isn't that grand all the same? And in one of the better rooms, at that, with a sea view."

"So they arrived two days early? Or was that the way they planned it, to surprise the family?"

"It was indeed, Patrick. So our lips must be sealed, Mary-Anne's too. She's back at waiting tables now that Doctor Gilmore has arrived. He'll be staying for a few days, so Mary-Anne will be home later this evening."

Maggie had hoped the mention of Mary-Anne would lead her into a conversation about the trouble Patrick seemed to be having with his wife, but there was such an awkward silence, she was unable to speak of it.

It was Patrick that spoke instead, "There's no need to fret, Maggie. I won't let the cat out of the bag, it would spoil the surprise for Thomas. So you met his wife then?"

"I did indeed. Oh, Lily's a grand girl, Patrick. And such a beauty. Why, our Thomas was as proud as a peacock when he introduced her to me."

Maggie prattled on as they walked but Patrick took in little of what she said. His thoughts were on a meeting, soon to be held in Cootehill, and he had set his heart on going. He had even convinced a handful of men from one of the factories in Dundalk to attend. If Catherine found out about it there would be hell to pay. She had made him promise to stay away from such groups and organizations.

The goals of The International Working Men's Association, more commonly known as the First International, were much the same as those espoused at that fateful meeting in Sheffield, when Patrick and his friends had been attacked by a gang sent to make trouble. In spite of him ending up with a knife in his side, put there by one of the assailants, the fight for the rights of the working man remained as close to Patrick's heart as ever.

All the talk about Home Rule in Paddy Mac's went over Patrick's head. He wondered if any of those landless fishermen really believed they would one day have a say in how the country should be governed. Even with the secret ballot being introduced, not enough men in Ireland were eligible to vote anyway, so as to bring about any great change.

To make matters worse, there had been a steady increase in rents throughout the country, due to the meagre harvests because of continuous bad weather. Those who had lived through the Great Hunger feared a return of desperate years and when not discussing politics, the talk would often turn to the lack of work on land and at sea.

CHAPTER THIRTEEN

The low hum of conversation coupled with the aroma of traditional Irish food, created a relaxing environment for Thomas and Lily after a stormy crossing of the Irish Sea. While waiting to board a steam packet to Dundalk, they had spent time with some of the McGrother family from Sunderland, who had travelled to Liverpool to meet up with them. Sailing on a smaller ship had been a lot more difficult for Thomas, who much preferred to have his feet on solid ground.

Lily, on the other hand, had enjoyed every minute of the journey, relishing each dip of the vessel after it had crested a wave – an action that forced Thomas to heave into a bucket.

"What did you make of my aunt Maggie, then?"

"Oh, she's adorable. If the rest of your family are at all like her, I will be more than happy to meet them. Hmm, have you tasted this ham?" Lily looked up and saw the paleness of her husband's face. "Sorry, my love. I forgot how delicate your stomach is this evening."

Glancing down at his plate, Thomas hoped the chef would not be too upset at the few mouthfuls he had managed to take. He made a mental note to compliment the food and explain his reason for being unable to finish the meal. His sister Mary-Anne had taken their order and she would understand how he was feeling.

Thomas had already introduced his wife to Mary-Anne and it was she who was serving their table. He had been pleasantly surprised to see his normally fractious sister smiling and friendly.

"And how did you find my sister Mary-Anne?"

"She seems very nice indeed. You have her eyes, Thomas, do they come from your father or your mother?"

"I'm not sure. You will have to tell me yourself after you've met them."

While Lily spoke warmly about his Aunt Rose and Uncle Owen, who had met them in Liverpool, Thomas watched Mary-Anne as she served a table directly behind his wife. There was something about the way the gentleman smiled at his sister that disturbed him. While Mary-Anne took the woman's order the man's napkin fell from the table, landing on the floor. Thomas could see him lean down to retrieve it but instead of doing so immediately, he curled his hand around Mary-Anne's slender ankle and ran it slowly up towards her calf.

The sound of Thomas's heavy chair hitting the floor as it upended caused the other diners to jump. As the offending man sat bolt upright, Mary-Anne swung round to see her brother standing, glaring in her direction, his chair lying on the floor behind him.

It wasn't the smile on her face, nor the pink tinge to her cheeks, that confused Thomas. It was the look in her eyes. A gaze that seconds before, had been upon a man seductively caressing her ankle.

Instinctively, Mary-Anne knew that her brother had witnessed the furtive display of affection she so craved from Doctor Gilmore. Excusing herself from his table, she walked over to Thomas and put her lips close to his ear. His

69

eyes were still trained on the man who had dared to touch his sister in such a disrespectful manner.

"Mind your own business, Thomas. I know how to look after myself. Now, sit down and behave," she whispered harshly to him.

One of the other diners had already picked up the chair and Thomas sank back down onto his seat.

"There you are, old chap," he poured some water into a glass. "Or do you think you would benefit from something a little stronger?"

Thomas shook his head and thanked the man. "I haven't been feeling too well. We had a rough crossing from Liverpool today. I'm not too good a sailor even when it's calm. Lily, would you give my apologies to the chef. Tell him I look forward to another one of his fine meals tomorrow, when my stomach has had a chance to settle."

As he stood up Mary-Anne smiled sweetly and suggested Lily accompany her brother to their room.

"I fear he may faint climbing the stairs. He is as white as the table linen, is he not? I'll see to it the chef gets your message, Thomas."

Lily stood and linked her arm through her husband's, "Yes, of course, Mary-Anne. You are quite right. Come, my love. Let's get you up to bed. It's been a long tiring day for both of us."

Having taken the remainder of the order from Mrs. Gilmore, Mary-Anne removed the plates from the table at which her brother and his wife had been seated. As she passed by the chef she noticed Thomas's untouched food and frowned.

"He said it wasn't to his liking, and that his *'mother could make a tastier meal blindfolded, with one hand tied behind her back.'* But that's my brother for you, never satisfied. Our ma's a fair enough cook, but not nearly as good as yourself, Chef," Mary-Anne watched with pleasure as her words sank in. "Don't you be fretting now, I'll have a word with our Thomas. I'll see that he behaves himself while he's here. We'll not be having any of his fancy airs and graces, will we? Even if he *is* a well-known writer in New York."

Once they were in the privacy of their room, Lily questioned her husband about his behaviour in the dining room. It was not something that Thomas could put into words, without sounding foolish.

"I was fully sure that I was about to bring up the few mouthfuls of food I had taken, Lily. I rose too quickly and even frightened myself with the noise of my chair falling over."

"I suppose it was embarrassing for you, my love. The whole room staring at you. But Thomas, why did you glare at your sister so? You had a very strange look to your face."

"Really, Lily. Have I not explained myself sufficiently to you? I am beginning to feel like a criminal, with all your questioning."

Thomas had begun to pace back and forth across the room, when a knock sounded on the door. He opened it wide to reveal Mary-Anne standing in the corridor.

"I've finished my work for the day and wanted to make sure you were faring well, Thomas," she said.

"Come in, Mary-Anne. Do come in and take a seat," Lily pulled her sister-in-law in by the hand.

"I think you could do with some air, Thomas. You still look quite pale. Maybe you should come home with me and surprise the family tonight, instead of tomorrow. Sure someone is bound to have seen you and word could get back before you have had a chance to see them first."

"Why that's a splendid suggestion, Mary-Anne. What do you say, Thomas? Shall we accompany your sister home? I'm sure I won't sleep a wink tonight, waiting for the morning to come."

Thomas agreed, partly because he didn't want to take a chance on their surprise being spoiled, but mostly because he had a longing to see his daughter, Eliza.

"But the children will be settled for the night, surely we should not risk disturbing them? They have school tomorrow, have they not?" asked Thomas.

"Ma will keep them home tomorrow. Your darling little girl shall want to spend every precious minute with her father, Thomas," Mary-Anne smiled sweetly in Lily's direction. "Eliza has her mother's sweet nature, rest her poor soul, and her grandmother's beauty. That's where our Thomas gets his handsome face, Lily. From our mother. But sure you'll see that for yourself when you meet her."

As Thomas walked to his parents' home, linked by his wife on one side and his sister on the other, he noticed how quiet the houses were. They hadn't passed by a soul on the way, which felt very odd to him.

"Where is everyone, Mary-Anne? The rain has stopped and I would have expected to find a few locals out and about, the hour isn't that late."

With a deep sigh, Mary-Anne explained how miserable their neighbours had become. The constant bad weather had devastated the crops, which meant the local fishermen had no farm labouring to supplement their income.

"If it weren't for the visitors the place would be as dead as a doornail. Sure it's thanks to them that I have a wage myself."

Mary-Anne looked around to make sure they were still alone, then leaned across Thomas so that Lily would hear her whispered words.

"I've heard some of the guests at the hotel remark on how atrocious the weather has been on their last few visits, and that if it keeps up they will head to the south of England, or even as far as France, to take the air. And I don't blame them one bit."

"I don't think it will come to that," said Thomas. "A lot of visitors have been coming here year after year. Why, even their grandparents used to come. It has become a family tradition for most of them, I don't think you need worry about losing your position at the hotel, Mary-Anne."

"Oh, that doesn't bother me at all, for I have other plans, but I cannot share them with you. Not yet, at least."

Having arrived at the McGrother home, the trio came to a halt in front of the gate. Lily cast her eyes across a small, tidy garden separated by a flagstone path that led to a red, freshly painted half-door. A column of small shrubs and herbs interspersed with large, white-washed stones ran along each side of the path.

Thomas stood back, manoeuvring his sister in front of him.

"You go on in first Mary-Anne and tell Ma that her hens are on the loose. That'll have her running out quick enough."

"Oh, Thomas, you're as mischievous as ever. She'll kill the both of us for tricking her so, but it will be worth it to see her face when she catches sight of you," Mary-Anne replied.

Lily was on edge with the prospect of coming face to face with a family that meant so much to her new husband. She fully expected to feel like an intruder and believed that it would take more than a short stay to become an accepted member of his family.

Mary came rushing out of the house wielding a broom and shouting that she had a good mind to let the fox get her troublesome hens. Thomas, who had been standing to one side of the doorway, waited until she had walked past him before calling to her.

"Ma, the hens are fine."

His mother stopped in her tracks and Thomas felt tears sting at the back of his eyes as he watched her drop the broom and slowly turn around.

"Heavens above, Thomas McGrother. Do you want to make my heart stop, frightening your poor old mother like that."

They stood taking in the sight of each other for all of five seconds, until Thomas rushed forward and scooped Mary into his arms. He swung her around twice before depositing her in front of his new wife, who had been watching from the other side of the doorway.

"Ma, this is Lily, your new daughter-in-law."

He has his mother's eyes, thought Lily, as she held out a hand and smiled at the woman who stood before her.

"I can see that you've made my son a very happy man. You've driven the sadness out of his letters, and judging by the big foolish grin he's wearing now, it's gone from his heart, too. You are more than welcome in our family, Lily, my dear."

The warmth in her mother-in-law's voice left the young woman speechless and close to tears. As Mary ignored the proffered hand to embrace her, Lily smiled with relief at Thomas who stood directly behind his mother. The light from the open door beamed across his face and she could see that his eyes were glistening. Like a wave suddenly appearing in a calm sea, the three of them were surrounded by the rest of the family and swept into the house.

CHAPTER FOURTEEN

A cool breeze blew through the slightly open window and the sound of waves pounding on the sand across from the hotel had a profound effect on Lily. She had left her bed to push up the sash and stood for a moment looking out at a moonlit, restless sea.

"I've never felt such passion as I did tonight, Thomas. It must be the sea air. I daresay you think me a woman of ill repute after that," she said, climbing back into her warm bed.

"And am I not to get any credit for arousing such emotion in you, Lily?" Thomas drew her close and felt the chill on her body.

"Oh, just a little, perhaps," she teased. "Does the pounding of the waves make your heart race, Thomas, as it does mine?"

Thinking about it, he realized that it had been a very long time since he had listened to that sound. It always reminded him of his childhood years in Blackrock.

"I suppose I must have heard the crash of waves on the shores of America, but I daresay I ignored them. They never made my heart race like it did tonight. But then, you played no small part yourself in that, my love," Thomas kissed her forehead. "What did you make of my family, Lily? They were all very taken with you."

"They are delightful, and made me feel so welcome, especially Mary-Anne, in spite of your warning about her. May I ask you something about Eliza, Thomas?"

"Ask me anything, my love, we must keep no secrets from each other."

"Would you like to bring her back to America with us? For I would dearly love to do so. She is an adorable child and took to me so readily. I would care for her as if she were my own, Thomas."

"I knew she would have that effect on you, Lily. That's why I never spoke of her joining us, I didn't want you to feel that my affections were divided. There is nothing I wish more in the world than to take Eliza with me, but I fear the time is not right. We must wait until we are more settled, with a permanent home and a steady wage. I'll speak to my father about it, for the thought of losing her would cause my mother too much grief, and I want to see her smile every day that I am here."

Thomas's line of thought drifted to earlier that evening, when his younger brother, Jamie, ran to fetch Catherine from her home.

"My sister Catherine did not seem to be quite herself. If I didn't know better, I would think she and Mary-Anne had exchanged personalities. How did you find her, Lily?

"She seemed a little preoccupied. Perhaps one of her little ones is unwell and it was playing on her mind. From our correspondence with her I was expecting to feel more welcome by Catherine than any other member of your family. In truth, Thomas, she made me feel most uncomfortable."

"It may be nothing more than what you said about one of the children being ill. It would be in her nature to keep silent about such a thing so as not to spoil the evening. We shall have to spend some time alone with Patrick and

Catherine. I would like to treat them to a supper here at the hotel, some evening."

Lily replied that it would be lovely for the four of them to get to know each other more intimately and she herself would like to spend time with Catherine alone, for the same reason. She instinctively felt that Thomas's older sister had a lot more troubling her that evening than a sick child.

That same night, in their home not too far from the hotel, the few words exchanged between Catherine and her husband were strained. Patrick had remained at the house as their children slept, while she and Maggie had followed Jamie to his home, unaware of the surprise that lay in store for them.

"Is Thomas keeping well?" asked Patrick.

"He is indeed, as is his wife. She seemed very much at ease surrounded by the family," replied Catherine.

"And your father? Did *he* appear to be *very much at ease* with her?"

"Yes, he seemed quite taken with Lily. Da is a very good judge of character and there are few people he truly cannot take to."

"Me being one of them," said Patrick.

"I'm off to my bed. I have to go to the hotel in the morning in place of Maggie, she is not too well of late. In fact, she has asked me if I would like to take her place there, as the stairs are becoming more difficult for her to climb," Catherine could see that Patrick was about to argue with her, so she cut him short. "I do not wish to discuss the matter with you tonight, Patrick."

Catherine turned her back to him, quickly undressed and climbed into her bed. Patrick was left struggling to find the right words that would convince his wife the children needed her at home. He slumped onto his chair by the fire, resigning himself to the fact that any argument along those lines would be futile. They needed the money and if Maggie wasn't able to continue at the hotel it made sense that Catherine should take her place. Half the family were already employed there, young Breege having been taken on the year before.

His eyes drew themselves from the glow of the fire and Patrick let them fall across the slender form lying in his bed. He knew that Catherine would not have fallen asleep already and couldn't bring himself to lie beside her with such a wall of silent frustration between them. Eventually, his aching muscles drove Patrick into the small room at the back of the house, where Maggie slept with the children.

His youngest child lay in the older woman's arms, both of them snoring softly, while Tom and Maisie slept back to back in the only other bed in the room. Patrick carefully lifted his daughter, taking her place beside his son. The feeling the young father loved most in the world swept over him as he lay Maisie on his chest. Tom instinctively turned in his sleep and moved closer to his father. It was only when his own children came along that Patrick could understand the determination of his father in keeping his motherless family together. By removing them from the workhouse after his wife's death and joining the mass of people taking a boat away from their homeland,

Thomas Gallagher had probably saved his children's lives.

A small hand reached up to Patrick's face, its fingers searching around his mouth, until they found the moustache that told Maisie she was in her father's arms. Without opening her eyes, the little girl sighed and settled back to sleep. Patrick knew if it came to it, he would not have to think twice about leaving Ireland for the sake of his children.

Financially, the family had been better off in England, but their living conditions had been far worse. Maggie's income from the hotel helped to supplement what Patrick managed to earn between fishing and labouring. He knew that it made sense for Catherine to take her aunt's place, if she could no longer keep up with the work, but such an arrangement did not sit well with Patrick. He was well aware of what his father-in-law would have to say about it and didn't relish giving him the satisfaction of having one more reason to admonish him.

James McGrother was of the opinion that a wife might help her husband in his work, as his own wife had done selling the fish he caught at market, but to clean another man's premises to bring a little money into the house, was a different matter entirely. Patrick had to admit to feeling the same way about it, but reminded himself that women had been working in factories and mills for years, and before that, had laboured alongside men in the fields. It was nothing new for a wife to earn money in her own right, it was just a matter of male pride. Patrick considered himself a modern man, and knew there would come a time for change, not just for men but women, too. It was a future he wished for his children and if he couldn't give it to them in his own country, then he would take them to wherever it was they might find it.

CHAPTER FIFTEEN

A crowd of people had gathered around a man standing on a wooden crate in Roden Place. Kelly's monument loomed behind him, a stark reminder of a courageous sea rescue just off the coast at Blackrock, which had cost the lives of four local men. Catherine had been a child when the Mary Stoddard ran aground but the memory of such a tragedy had stayed with her into adulthood.

The very articulate man standing in front of the monument was beginning to attract even more people, but his speech was constantly interrupted by two hecklers trying their best to shout him down. Patrick ran forward and grabbed hold of their scruffy jackets. Dragging them from the centre of the crowd, he chased them away, shouting abuse after them. Catherine saw the man on the box tip his hat to her husband before carrying on with his speech.

"Do you know him?" she whispered, when he returned to her side.

"I was supposed to be here today to give him my support. He will think it odd if I were to walk away now," said Patrick.

Thomas spoke quietly to Lily, who nodded and moved nearer to Catherine, linking her arm, "Why don't you and I have a look at the fabric in that shop window over there, and leave the men to their own devices for a while?"

"Why Lily, that's a splendid idea. What do you say, Patrick?" Thomas winked at his brother-in-law.

Catherine didn't even try to hide the accusing glare she gave her husband, but Patrick was happy to agree with the suggestion and ignored her.

"But the shop is closed," said Catherine.

"I can see a woman looking into the street from the window above," noted Patrick. "If she sees you approach I daresay she won't be long in opening the door. Maisie could do with a new pinafore," he reached into his pocket.

"No, no, Patrick. It shall be a gift from us. Thomas has always said what a neat seamstress his sister is. I would love to help you choose some fabric, Catherine," said Lily.

For a few seconds it looked as if the young mother would refuse the offer, but she had never been one to make a scene and her face relaxed into a smile.

"It's very kind of you both to make such a gesture. Maisie will be delighted, thank you."

The men watched as the women crossed the street. It wasn't long before the shop door opened and the two young women had disappeared from view.

"If I know my wife, they will be in there for as long as the speech goes on," Thomas nodded in the direction of the crowd. "Shall we join the onlookers in the meantime?"

Patrick was impressed by the younger man's maturity but worried that trouble might erupt among the growing crowd.

"I fear there could be more hecklers still mingling, waiting for an opportunity to cause trouble. I would not like any harm to come to you, Thomas. We can listen from where we stand."

"Come now, Patrick, I have been swept up in rioting crowds, much larger than this one, and have managed to survive. I think I can handle a wee bit of trouble if it rears its ugly head."

Thomas was already at the edge of the men surrounding the speaker.

"Let's stay here, where we can get away more easily at the first sign of a riot." said Patrick.

Touched by his brother-in-law's concern, Thomas smiled and removed a small notebook and pencil from his pocket.

"My editor will be pleased to see this report. The Irish in New York are very active in politics. Sure who could blame them, Patrick? Even their children who were born there, and have never set foot on Irish soil, are as enthusiastic as their parents."

Patrick's attention had been drawn to a doorway where two priests stood in the shadows, observing the crowd. He had seen the two hecklers run in that direction earlier and wondered if they had paid them to disrupt the speech.

"Look over yonder, Thomas. The Church is very nervous about the First International. The bishops fear it a threat to their flock."

"It won't be an easy task to bring about change, but it will come, Patrick, from small beginnings such as this."

As the speech was winding down, three young boys passed through the crowd, dispensing leaflets. One of them greeted Patrick by name as he walked by.

"He seems to know you but he never offered you a handbill, is that because you are already involved?" asked Thomas.

"I am, but not as much as I would like to be. Not a word to Catherine, mind. She cannot understand why I would risk bringing trouble upon my shoulders when I'm not even a factory worker."

"Is that why she has taken on such a sombre nature, Patrick, or is there more to it? She is not the sister I grew up with."

"She is not the woman I married either. But you will have to ask her yourself why that is, Thomas. I have no wish to bring any more of her wrath upon my head."

The speaker came up to the two men and shook their hands while Patrick introduced him to his brother-in-law.

"Are you planning on attending the rally in Cootehill?" he asked.

Before Patrick could say a word Thomas said that he was, "We shall both be there, even if not another soul from Louth attends."

"And you'd be very welcome. You must come to my home for a meal afterwards, unless you have other plans," the man looked behind where the three boys with the handbills continued offering them to passers-by.

"I had best be getting my sons home, my wife worries that some harm might come to them should there be any trouble. I'm much obliged to you, Patrick, for stepping in there when you did. Those hecklers could have drawn the militia down on us if a fight had broken out."

The men shook hands once more before parting and as soon as they were alone, Thomas saw their wives emerging from the shop carrying brown paper parcels tied up with twine.

"I hope we haven't kept you waiting too long, but the lady in the shop insisted that we have tea with her. Is that usual in Ireland? She opened her shop especially for us, and it a bank holiday today," said Lily.

"It was because you made so many purchases. I daresay it's been a long time since she sold so much in one day. Even the gentry are tightening their purse strings of late," said Catherine.

As the two young husbands took the parcels from their wives Thomas felt the weight of them and declared that he was going to sew up his purse the next time Lily was in sight of a shop.

"I'm sure that poor woman thought we would come to blows on her premises," said Catherine. "No matter how much I argued against it, your wife continued to buy more and more fabric. I hope you have a prepaid ticket home, Thomas, or you may be staying here a lot longer than planned."

Later that evening, Thomas watched his sister relax as she chatted to them, the old familiar sparkle back in her eyes. He was relieved that Mary-Anne was not on duty in the dining room as her presence might have generated an uneasy atmosphere at their table.

When they had finished eating, Thomas suggested a stroll through the village, as the evening was still bright and there wasn't even a hint of rain in the air. Patrick was taking the boat out that night and had to return home to make preparations.

"You'll come with us, won't you, Catherine?" asked Lily.

"Of course she will, sure isn't Maggie there with the children," said Patrick.

"That settles it so, I'll be the envy of all the men in the village with a beautiful woman on each arm," Thomas smiled as his wife and sister linked his arms.

Patrick listened to their laughter as the trio walked away and hoped that Catherine's good spirits would last. It had been a long time since he had heard such lightness in her voice.

Thomas was thinking along the same lines as his brother-in-law as he matched his step to the two young women at his side. While Catherine leaned across him to whisper something to Lily, three figures coming towards them caught his eye. He recognized Mary-Anne straight away but it took a little longer to identify the couple she was with. The woman walking between his sister and the tall, large framed man seemed frail. Her arms were linked through her companions on each side of her for support.

Catherine felt Thomas come to a halt and looked up to see Mary-Anne smiling at them. Introductions were made and small talk about the weather and fresh sea air ensued.

"You will be the first in the family to hear my good news," Mary-Anne announced. "Doctor Gilmore has taken a house for the summer here in Blackrock and I shall be live-in companion to Mrs. Gilmore while they are here."

Catherine feared the thumping of her heart would be heard, it felt so strong. A sharp pain shot across her chest and she doubled over. Thomas and Lily sat her on the sea wall and Doctor Gilmore quickly stepped in front of her, telling everyone to give her some space. She could feel his hands loosening the buttons at her throat and pulled them away in panic and disgust. "Leave me alone," she hissed into his face.

"Now, now, my dear. I am a doctor after all. Surely you can't have forgotten me already?" he whispered back.

Thomas could see how upset his sister had become and sensed that something was wrong with the scene before him. He placed a hand on Gilmore's shoulder and suggested that he, too, give her some space.

"Thank you for your concern, sir, but my sister was never one to enjoy being the centre of attention. I fear we may gather a crowd around her if you make such a fuss and that will only add to her distress."

Gilmore stared back at the younger man and looked as if he was about to argue. Instead, he nodded and bid them a good evening. "Come, my dear," he offered an arm to his wife, "We must finish our walk before it gets any cooler. It will not do for you to breathe in the air if it is chilled. Is that not so, Mary-Anne?"

"It is, Doctor Gilmore, and I shall be mindful of that while you are away, you need have no fear," Mary-Anne assured him.

She smiled at Thomas and told him in a voice loud enough for Catherine to hear, that she would be staying in the Gilmore's rented house that evening and would collect her belongings from home the next day.

"Have you spoken with our parents of this arrangement?" asked Thomas.

"Don't ask such a foolish question. I'm a grown woman, I do *not* need anyone's permission before I make a decision. Ma will be delighted for me to be a companion to Mrs. Gilmore," Mary-Anne shot a defiant look at Catherine. "Much better than cleaning floors and changing bed linen for a meagre wage."

Thomas watched on in frustration as Mary-Anne walked away from them. Loud sobbing erupting from Catherine took him by surprise and he knew immediately that something much more serious than sibling rivalry had reduced her to such a state. Lily was at Catherine's side, holding her hand and speaking quietly to her.

The only discreet place that Thomas could think of bringing his sister to, was back to their hotel room, so he took her by the elbow and guided her across the street towards the entrance. Lily followed behind, explaining to those giving them curious glances that her sister-in-law had taken ill. She asked that some tea and a measure of whiskey be sent to their room.

Once Catherine had let her emotions free, there was no stopping them. She cried so hard that Lily suggest they leave her on their bed until her energy was spent.

Thomas walked across to the window and looked along the street but could see no sign of Mary-Anne and the Gilmores. Replaying in his head, the scene that had caused Catherine so much distress, Thomas allowed his eyes to rest for a while on the changing colours of the sea in the sun's fading light. He never even turned around when the knock came on the door, announcing room service. It was Lily who took in the tray.

Catherine's sobs were easing somewhat and she raised herself into a sitting position, dabbing her eyes with the cold wet cloth that her sister-in-law had given her.

When Lily's arms encircled his waist and he felt the press of her face against his back, Thomas sighed and turned to embrace his wife. He glanced across the room and could see that Catherine was beginning to regain control of herself. In a low voice, he asked Lily what they should do next.

"I think that you should pay a visit to your Aunt Maggie, Thomas, and tell her that you have given myself and Catherine some time alone to become better acquainted," whispered Lily.

"Good suggestion, my love. I fear that something very serious is troubling her. Perhaps she will confide in you."

Thomas kissed Lily's forehead before crossing to the bed to sit beside his sister. She allowed him to take hold of one of her hands.

"I know you may not wish to confide in me, Catherine, but it isn't good to keep such pain locked up inside of you. Perhaps you and Lily should spend a wee bit of time alone, while I pay Aunt Maggie a visit," Thomas was relieved to see his sister nod in agreement. "You know what she is like, I may be there till midnight listening to all of her news. On my return, whenever you are ready to face the walk home, I shall accompany you."

Thomas kissed the top of his sister's head and squeezed Lily's hand before leaving the room.

"Would you like me to pour the tea, Catherine?"

"Please, Lily. I could do with a sup. I don't know what came over me. I have never before made such a show of myself in the street. What will people think of me?"

Lily poured a drop of whiskey into the sweetened tea, before handing it to her sister-in-law.

"I explained to one or two people that you had taken ill, so no doubt that will satisfy their curiosity," Lily thought for a moment about her next question.

"But I do not think that explanation will be sufficient for your brother. He will worry over it until you confide in him. Is there anything I can do to help, Catherine? I can assure you, I never betray a confidence. If only you knew me better, you would understand why that is."

Catherine was not sure if it was the kindness in Lily's voice or the cosiness of the room, or even the small amount of whiskey in her tea, that melted her reserve. Once she began to share some of her fears, the whole sorry account of her traumatic encounter with Gilmore some years before, came flooding out. She was incapable of holding anything back, in spite of a burning humiliation colouring her cheeks.

Poor Lily had not expected to hear the anguish and torment that her sister-in-law had been carrying around for so many years. She had thought it would be a marital problem of some sort that would be divulged, the usual one being of a husband's infidelity. As Catherine continued to speak, Lily found it hard to focus on her words and wished that Thomas had not left her alone with his sister.

"So, do you see why I cannot tell Patrick why I am so against Mary-Anne being in the company of such a man, never mind living in the same house as him?"

Lily put her arms around Catherine and held her close. Any feelings of regret she had about listening to such a litany of distressing events left her instantly. Instead, she was filled with sympathy and love for the young woman sitting on the bed beside her.

"I do, Catherine, I do. We cannot tell Thomas of this either. Not just yet, while that wretched man is here in the village. I know for sure he would not be able to restrain himself from thrashing that beast to within an inch of his life. I'm sorry, love, but I'm afraid I may not be much help to you in offering any suggestions."

Having regained her composure, Catherine patted the back of Lily's hand and assured her that she was not expecting anything from her.

"You've given me the chance to share a terrible secret that haunts me. If I had been within earshot of my Aunt Rose, you would not have had to suffer such an outburst. It's me who should be apologizing to you. When Thomas returns I will let him walk me home and on the way, I'll tell him that I worry about Mary-Anne's jealousy of my marriage. He's well aware of her belief that I took Patrick away from her, so it shall not be too difficult to convince him that we have been having our usual sisterly conflict."

CHAPTER SIXTEEN

As Martin Butler's five young children left the table, they each grabbed one more slice of bread and laughed while their father pretended to admonish them for their greed.

"Here, young man," he said to a ragged boy standing on the street just outside their open door, "Take this last slice for yourself. You can't be following my lot around with your mouth hanging open with the hunger and them stuffing their gobs."

The young boy ran forward, a cheerful smile brightening up his grubby face. "Bless you Mr. Butler. Your wife makes the best bread in the whole of Cavan. I do smell it when I'm in me bed at night. Torments me it does but it's better than the stink coming from the dung heaps in the yard."

"Off with you now, before I change my mind about the bread," said Martin.

"That young fella lives at the back of our house. You wouldn't think to look at him he was working now, would you? Every farthing goes to his ma. She has three of her six young ones working and he's the eldest, at nine. Every penny they earn has to feed them. Their da hands up enough for the rent and drinks the rest."

"The same thing happens back in America," said Thomas. "There are some unfortunates who settle in the cities and succumb to the demon drink. It dulls the anguish they feel at being trapped. So many arrive there full of hope, lured by the promise of a better life, and many of them do make a life for themselves. The ones who don't, or are unable to, might as well have stayed at home."

"You have a fine brood yourself, Martin, like steps of stairs they are. What age is your eldest lad?" asked Patrick.

"Ten and still in school," Martin looked around his meagre possessions in the small parlour of his home. "And he'll be staying there for another year, if I have my way. After that, I think we will all be taking the boat to America. I have two sisters there and they've been saving for our tickets. I fear that justice for the likes of us will be better fought on foreign soil, than here in Ireland."

Martin had agreed to be interviewed by Thomas for his paper, on the condition that his name not be disclosed. Anonymously, he could vividly describe the sorry state of affairs for many who worked hard all week, yet never earned enough to free their families from poverty. For those who lived in the cities, the children they bore became more factory fodder, if they were 'fortunate' enough to gain employment, and the cycle went on. In rural areas there was less chance of finding regular employment, forcing both men and women to emigrate.

As they made their way towards the train station, having bade farewell to Martin and his family, Thomas took a mental note of the children following them. He could just as easily have been in the slums of Liverpool, London or New York, the scene was the same. His old trick of detaching himself from his surroundings quickly kicked in, before any trace of emotion could reach his heart. Thomas had learned how to do so, in order to carry out his work as a journalist. He knew those feelings never truly went away but stored themselves inside, waiting to be released. It was Lily who had saved him from drinking himself into an early grave.

Lily always joked at how Thomas had arrived like a knight in shining armour and rescued her from a life that she had made numerous unsuccessful attempts to escape from. She eventually planned the only sure way out and had accepted her fate with a calm heart. Thomas stopped her, as she was about to throw herself into the Hudson River.

Keeping pace with Thomas, Patrick vocally deplored the malnourished condition of some of the children, but his protests landed on deaf ears. To keep his feelings in check, Thomas tried to catch sight of any child wearing shoes or boots, but were none to be found. Even fabric crudely wrapped around their feet would have been something. He himself had always loved to be barefoot as a child in Blackrock, with either grass or sand under his feet. In Sunderland it was a different story and he was thankful that his cousins passed on their boots to him when they outgrew them. Thomas doubted his younger sisters were happy whenever they in turn inherited his third or fourth hand boots. As they grew older, that happened less often and as soon as Catherine and himself began to bring in some extra money, their younger siblings rarely went barefoot.

Patrick was glad to be sitting on the train and heading home, although he knew that there would be no welcoming smile from Catherine awaiting him.

"Will you be fishing tonight, Patrick?" asked Thomas.

"As long as the weather behaves, I'll be out. What do you think of your wee Jamie becoming a fisherman?"

"That was no surprise, it's all he has ever wanted to do. He's grateful to you for speeding things up. If you hadn't promised him a place on your crew, Da would have waited much longer. Is it true that you can swim, Patrick?"

"Aye, it is. But I wonder if that's more of a curse than a blessing."

"I'm sure young Petey Halpin thinks it a blessing. He told me you'd taught him to swim, not long after you saved him from drowning. Would you do the same for our Jamie, Patrick?"

"I thought about it, but myself and your da don't see eye to eye on too many things, Thomas. I have enough trouble keeping on the right side of my wife without bringing her father's wrath upon my head, too."

"If becoming involved in worker's rights will come between you, then think carefully about what you commit to, Patrick. There are other ways to show support without having to attend meetings and rallies. Catherine's fear for your safety is not unwarranted. I've seen too many peaceful protests turn into angry mobs. Can you take the chance of being arrested, or worse, with a young family to provide for?"

"How can you say that, when you have a wife and daughter yourself?" Patrick was defensive.

"Eliza is here in Ireland and I have a small life insurance policy that will go to both of them in the event of my death," replied Thomas. "Besides, I'm considering a more permanent position, with another periodical, as an editor. Lily wants to put down roots and make a proper home for us, I'm ready now to do that. Please don't speak of this to my family, Patrick. Ma will fear that I'm preparing to take Eliza away from her. When the time comes and she is old enough to make such a decision, I want her to have a home to come to, if she so wishes."

"Have no fear, I won't even speak of it to Catherine – she may be tempted to interfere. I'm not sure I know my own wife any more, Thomas."

"Something is deeply disturbing her, Patrick. I know she is against your involvement with the First International, but I feel that Mary-Anne is causing her more anxiety than your activities. Perhaps she will confide in Lily before the end of our stay. Having the attention of a sympathetic ear may be enough to bring back the old Catherine."

Both men were very quiet on the return journey, with Thomas making notes in his journal and Patrick deep in thought about his wife's unhappiness.

The two mile walk home from Dundalk reminded Thomas of his childhood ventures into the town, in the days before his father owned a donkey.

"Would you ever consider coming to America, yourself?" he asked.

Patrick admitted that it had crossed his mind on numerous occasions, particularly since his return to Ireland.

"It's your sister you should be putting that question to. If she asked me to go, I'd be packed and ready tomorrow. But Catherine is too much like her father. How is it that you had the courage to move so far from home and family, and leave your wee one behind like that?"

Thomas's long silence caused Patrick to think he had offended him.

"I'm sorry. I should not have asked such a personal question, it was wrong of me."

"No, no, Patrick. I haven't taken offense. I was just thinking on what you said and how best to answer you. It wasn't courageous of me at all. In order to be courageous you must be in fear, but I was never anxious about leaving, nor about what lay ahead. To be truthful, Patrick, I was numb inside. When you feel that way, it's easy to make a decision that would have otherwise been formidable. Besides, I had an offer of employment and that made it easier to go."

"What made you take an interest in writing? It's a strange manner of work for a fisherman's son."

"Ah, Patrick, I was always one for words, even as a child. I remember the master in school telling me I could be a great poet, if I put my mind to it. But Ma always said *the greater the poet, the emptier the stomach.*"

"What did she mean by that?" asked Patrick.

"I think she meant that, too much time spent writing instead of labouring would mean less money in the pocket. If I was to depend on fishing for my livelihood I would have starved long ago, for I have never had the stomach for a boat. There is a newspaper cutting in the tin box where Da keeps all his letters and I used to ask him to read it to me when I was a child. It was written by a journalist called Alexander Somerville, about the terrible conditions in Ireland at the time of the great famine. I met him last year in Toronto, when I was sent there by my editor. He's a big man with a strange temperament. I asked him if he remembered writing about Mary McGrother's trip to Sunderland in 1847 and do you know what he said to me? He told me he couldn't even remember what he had breakfasted on that morning. Then he laughed heartily and slapped me on the back, before walking away."

"I never heard that story before, about your ma meeting someone like him," said Patrick.

"His carriage knocked her off her feet on one of her visits to England and his wife insisted she join them for a meal. Somerville asked Ma if she would allow him to publish her story and he paid her well for it. I think that must have planted the seed in me, to become a writer one day."

"I lost my mother at that time. That's why we went to England. My father never spoke of the hardship. Not many do, even now, as if it was of their own making, something to be ashamed of," said Patrick.

"That's why I believe in the power of words. You should learn to read, Patrick. It would open up the world to you."

"Aye, maybe you're right about that. I'll think on it, Thomas."

CHAPTER SEVENTEEN

Mrs. Gilmore's attention was constantly drawn towards the birds flitting from tree to tree in the tiny private garden, where she sat with her husband. Doctor Gilmore patted the seat beside him, gesturing for Mary-Anne to join them for some afternoon tea and that meant only one thing.

She knew it was wrong, but Mary-Anne couldn't help herself. Gilmore's attempts to touch her in an inappropriate manner had become a game to them both. Mary-Anne began to crave the sensation caused by such furtive behaviour. At night she lay in a bed so soft, compared to the one she normally shared with her sister Breege, that it caused her to feel even more lascivious. She had only been three days in the house with Doctor Gilmore and his wife, but had fallen asleep each night disappointed he had not come to her room.

Mary-Anne's heightened emotions did not go unnoticed by her mother. She questioned her daughters about any men that their sister might be keeping company with. Even Maggie was interrogated on the subject.

"If Mary-Anne has a suitor she will tell us in her own good time. She's a grown woman, after all, Mary. You'll have to cut her free from your apron strings sooner or later," said Maggie.

"I still see her as a girl. I can't help it – she was such a sickly child. Even now, her chest is not good in damp weather. Sure, our Breege is much more of a woman than Mary-Anne will ever be. You said that to me, yourself, only last week did you not?"

"Aye, I did indeed, Mary. And I still stand by it. But Mary-Anne is cunning, and well able to mind herself. So stop your fretting now, and we'll go outside and weed that garden of yours, while the day is fine. We haven't been blessed with too many dry days this year, more's the pity."

James, awake in the loft bedroom overhead, had heard every word of the conversation. He had been catching up on his sleep, having spent the night fishing on Matthew Clarke's boat. He looked across at his youngest, Jamie, and wondered where the years had gone. Downstairs his wife and sister were discussing their grown up daughters and calling them women, while young Jamie, was already a fisherman, barely into his teens.

'I'm getting old,' James thought as he eased his aching body into action. Once on his feet and moving about, he began to feel less stiff and by the time he had reached the bottom of the stairs he felt ten years younger. Jamie's loud snores from the room upstairs could be heard throughout the quiet house. Letting him have his sleep, his father decided against waking him up with a cup of tea. Having the parlour to himself was a rare thing for James and he intended making the most of it.

Taking a newspaper from a drawer in the dresser, James swung the large black kettle directly over the fire and waited for the water to come back to a boil. He knew the plate of bread on the table had been left there by Mary, for himself and Jamie. The thought struck him that

101

he should go out and help the women in the garden, but he dismissed it immediately. He was sure they would rather have the time to talk freely between themselves, without a man hovering around them.

As soon as his breakfast was over and a second cup of tea poured out, James unfolded the paper. He was not one for eating and reading at the same time, so the anticipation of the latest news to be unveiled had him ready to devour every word in front of his eyes. A voice calling to him from outside cut into a report about an armed robbery in one of the estate houses in a nearby county. James looked over the paper to see Catherine leaning on the closed part of the half-door, smiling at him.

"Am I disturbing your bit of peace and quiet, Da?"

Sighing, James folded his paper and laid it on the table. He still had a soft spot for his eldest and always enjoyed her company.

"Not at all, girl. Come in and sit yourself down, or is it your ma you're wanting to see?" James was pouring her some tea as he spoke.

"No Da, I've already been round the back. Herself and Maggie are like work horses out there, I was getting tired just looking at them. I think I was more in the way when I tried to help them with the weeding. They kept watching me in case I pulled up the wrong plant," Catherine sipped the hot tea. "Thank you, Da. Thirsty work, gardening, isn't it?"

They both laughed, but James noticed a sadness in his daughter's eyes. He waited for her to say something but she just stared at the half open door and seemed lost in thought.

"Are all the children faring well, love?" he asked.

"They are, Da. Fit as fiddles the three of them. Thomas and Lily have taken them to play on the sand, now that the tide is out. They've taken a right shine to their new auntie. What do you make of her, yourself?" Catherine asked.

"She seems a fine young woman, from what I can see. Thomas has been blessed twice with good women, and him still so young."

"Do you feel blessed too? Or are the women in your life more of a curse to you?"

James was taken aback at the bitterness in his daughter's tone. She was the last person he would have expected to ask such a question, considering how close they had always been.

"Of course I feel blessed. What reason have I ever given you to think otherwise?"

Catherine could hear the hurt in his voice and immediately apologized, giving the excuse of a bad night's sleep for her sharpness.

"Why do you avoid my home so, Da? Is it because of Patrick?" the question was out before she could stop herself.

An awkward silence followed, while James busied himself pouring more tea into their half-filled cups.

"I cannot lie to you, Catherine. No matter how much I try, I don't seem to be able to warm to that man of yours. Surely that's a common enough feeling between men, when one of them takes away the other's daughter," said James.

The two of them sat looking at each other across the table and Catherine could see how much her father loved her, just from the expression on his face. The silence in the house added to the intensity of the moment and she had an overwhelming urge to tell him about the terrible secret she had been living with for such a long time. One that she could never share with her husband.

A loud crying broke the silence between them and Catherine jumped up from her chair, just as Lily appeared at the gate in front of the house. She was carrying Ellen, who was holding out her arms towards her mother.

"She fell and scratched her palms. I couldn't stop her crying. I'm sure she didn't hit her head," said Lily.

Catherine kissed the scratches on her toddler's small hands and was cuddling her close, when Maggie and Mary ran in from the garden.

"Merciful heaven, what ails the child? She sounds like a stuck pig," said Maggie.

At the sound of the older woman's voice, Ellen pulled away from her mother, stretched out her arms and displayed the bright red marks on her upturned hands.

"Ah you poor wee mite," consoled Maggie, taking the child from her mother. "Sit down here on my old rickety knee and tell us all about it."

"Is Thomas not with you?" asked Catherine.

"We met up with Patrick and I told the two of them to go to Paddy Mac's and have a drink while I stayed with the children. I'm sorry for letting Ellen hurt herself, I shouldn't have let her run around so much, should I?"

"Of course you should. That's not the first fall she's had and it won't be the last. Will it, my wee treasure?" Maggie tickled the child on her lap.

Young Jamie appeared at the foot of the stairs, woken by the loud crying, and Mary sent him to Paddy Mac's to fetch Thomas and Patrick.

"Tell them to come up and eat their meal with the rest of the family, while we are still all together," Mary smiled sadly at Lily.

By the time the two men arrived back with Jamie, the table had been set. The food prepared earlier that morning sat waiting for them, steaming potatoes, breaking out of their skins, cabbage fresh from the garden and two boiled chickens.

James looked at the meat, then caught his wife's eye and smiled, "Two more hens past their prime, I see," he tickled his granddaughter, Maisie, under the chin. "You'll come to visit me one of these days and your granny will have me in the pot, with some of her herbs and a few onions. Do you think I'll taste as nice as those old hens there?"

Maisie hugged her grandfather and made her grandmother promise never to cook him. The laughter and joking around the table sent a warm feeling through James and he made a promise to himself to put more effort into liking his son-in-law. It wasn't in him to bear grudges, especially for such a long period of time. Just when he was thinking along those lines, Patrick opened his mouth and ruined the moment.

"Do you think it right that a pair of hens, that you reared yourself, and a serving of vegetables should be considered a feast?" the question was addressed to no one in particular.

"Are you complaining about the food, or is it the company that bothers you?" asked James.

Even little Ellen fell silent, as the two men stared at each other.

"I'm not complaining. The food is the best that anyone could ask for. I'm saying that a hard-working man should be able to provide such a meal for his family every day," Patrick replied, holding the older man's steady gaze.

"I see. So I take it you do not consider me a hard-working man?"

"Of course I do, James. There's few men put more work into a week than yourself. Should you not see more fruit for your labour? Or are you satisfied with the meagre payment you are given for a well-built wall or an outhouse?"

"Times are hard these days, for farmers and landlords alike. The weather has been wreaking havoc on the crops. There's not much money in anyone's pocket of late – even the landlords'," said Thomas. "Why not leave this conversation for later, over a drink at Paddy Mac's. Judging by the wind that's come up I doubt either of you will be fishing tonight."

The women were grateful for Thomas's words. James and Patrick continued to stare at each other for a few more seconds, like opponents in a stand-off.

"I am not the enemy, James. Thomas is right and I apologize for bringing such serious talk to the table," Patrick turned to his son and ruffled his hair. "Why not give us one of your favourite songs to cheer us all up again, son."

"But Ma always says I'm not to speak with my mouth full."

"Ah, but she never said anything about singing with it full, did she?"

The children all laughed at their father's joke and the tension immediately left the room. A genuine smile even appeared on James's face, but one person remained ill at ease. Catherine watched as her husband playfully teased his children and wondered why he would make light of the manners she tried to teach them. She feared that something was brewing inside him and knew it was only a matter of time before it came out. When that happened there would be no holding him back.

CHAPTER EIGHTEEN

Doctor Gilmore had just two days left of his visit to Blackrock before returning to England. The hospital where he worked had been very understanding of his situation with his wife's illness, as long as he didn't take advantage of them. It was agreed that he should take one week off in four, while Mrs. Gilmore recuperated in Ireland.

Having Mary-Anne McGrother stay in the rented house was part of his plan to put pressure on her sister, Catherine. He knew that she had taken her aunt's place in the Blackrock Hotel and thanks to the idle talk of her sister, he was even aware of which days he could find her there. As Doctor Gilmore massaged his favourite cologne into his cheeks and throat, he admired his youthful appearance. The man looking back at him from the mirror over the mantelpiece of his small bedroom, although in his mid-forties, could have been ten years younger.

Gilmore had given his wife the larger room and Mary-Anne the middle-sized one, preferring the quietness at the back of the house. The birds singing in a tree outside his window would normally have irritated him and forced him to shut it tight, but his thoughts of Catherine brought a calmness and tolerance that belied the quick-tempered character he had been since childhood. Waiting for the right time to put his plan into action had taught him patience, something his father had never been able to do.

Having left the quiet house, careful not to disturb the two sleeping women, Doctor Gilmore made his way to the hotel. He knew that Catherine would be found changing beds and gathering laundry. He was also well aware of her unhappiness with her marriage, a fact that her sister Mary-Anne had attested to, on more than one occasion.

On the pretext of choosing a room for some guests that may be visiting the area, Gilmore had been given the keys to inspect some of the empty rooms.

"Are you sure you don't need me to accompany you, sir?" asked the man at reception.

"Not at all, I've stayed here myself, so I'm quite familiar with this hotel. I can see you are busy so I'll let you get on with your work."

"Oh, well, if you need anything, one of the cleaners is up there. She'll be able to answer any questions you might have concerning the rooms," the man called out after the doctor.

Climbing the stairs to put the last part of his plan into action, Gilmore could feel his pulse quicken with anticipation. It would only be a matter of minutes before a scene he had played over and over in his head became a reality. How would Catherine, so unhappy with a husband who neglected her for his radical friends, react?

'Her son's real father is about to extend a very generous hand to her,' thought Gilmore. 'How can she refuse?'

From halfway down the corridor the sound of soft humming could be heard and as he approached an open door Gilmore saw Catherine, her back turned to him, lifting a pile of sheets from a bed. He stepped into the room and closed the door.

"I'm sorry, I'm almost finished here . . ."

Catherine turned and froze at the scene that met her eyes.

Gilmore was leaning against the door, holding up a bunch of keys.

"I'm looking for a couple of rooms that might suit my friends on their visit here. I was told you may be of assistance in helping me choose them, Catherine."

Gilmore didn't move an inch as his terrified captive backed away towards the window. Dropping the bed linen onto the floor, Catherine pushed up the sash wide enough to climb through.

"If you come one step closer, I'll jump. I mean it."

"Don't be foolish, woman. The most damage you are likely to do is break both of your legs and how would that help your children. I believe that if it were not for the work you have in this establishment, your family would starve – or so your sister tells me," said Gilmore.

"You cannot believe a word Mary-Anne says. She is well known for her wild imagination and tall tales," Catherine was beginning to feel more in control beside the open window.

"Ah yes. Her vivid imagination. Shall I tell you about Mary-Anne's latest fantasy?" Gilmore went on in spite of Catherine firmly shaking her head at him. "The poor girl thinks that I may have an interest in her, beyond that of an employer."

Gilmore moved to the bed and Catherine sat on the window frame, neither one taking an eye

110

off the other. The doctor was savouring every second of her discomfort.

"She really is a very pretty girl, you know. Almost as pretty as you. What makes you far superior is the combination of beauty and intelligence – and the fact that you produce fine healthy offspring."

"What have my children got to do with you?" Catherine's fear was quickly replaced with anger.

"Come come, my dear. Have you forgotten young Tom's lineage? We both know that I am his father. The trouble is, your husband has not been made aware of that fact yet, has he?"

"What is it you want? It had better not be my son, for you will never have him."

The doctor walked around the bed to sit on the side nearest the window. Catherine had already made her mind up to scream, should he lay a hand on her and felt braver as a result.

"My wife has asked Mary-Anne to accompany her back to England at the end of the summer, to live as her companion. Mrs. Gilmore is quite taken with your sister. She feels very lonely throughout the long winter days, confined to the house due to inclement weather. I cannot give her the attention she needs as I must attend to my work at the hospital. Your sister has agreed to discuss it with your parents, but her excitement at the offer was plain to see."

The thought of Mary-Anne living so far away brought mixed emotions to Catherine. The fear that Gilmore would take advantage of her sister conflicted with a sense of relief, at no longer having to put up with hurtful remarks and sly threats. With Mary-Anne out of the way,

Catherine's relationship with Patrick might improve immensely. It may have been a selfish reason that influenced her next words but they had the desired effect on her tormentor.

"What a wonderful opportunity for Mary-Anne, your wife's offer is most generous. I cannot see why my parents would stand in her way," Catherine sounded much more positive than she felt.

Gilmore was in front of her in one stride and grabbed her by the elbows, pulling her up so close she could smell the old familiar cologne. The combination of his scent and his touch, made Catherine retch and she felt the sting of bile at the back of her throat. Turning her head to look in desperation at the street below, she saw one of her neighbours passing by and shouted out to her. As quickly as her assailant had grabbed hold of her, he let her go and stepped backwards, away from the window. Catherine continued to exchange greetings with the woman until she felt a tug at her skirt.

"I can see that I'm wasting my time. You need have no fear of me taking your son. And whatever generosity I was about to bestow on him will not be forthcoming, after your little display this morning. I will not give you another opportunity to insult me again. Good day to you, Mrs. Gallagher."

Catherine stood by the window and watched until she caught sight of Gilmore's tall figure enter the street below. It was only when he had walked far enough away to be out of her view that she could breathe easy. The rest of her working day passed in a blur for Catherine and it wasn't until she had to leave the hotel to walk home, that she once again felt her heart beat rapidly in her chest. What if Gilmore was waiting to accost her? Worse still, follow her home to make a scene with her husband present, or to snatch her son. The last thought set Catherine's legs in motion and her step quickened the nearer she got to her house.

A great roar of laughter told the frantic young woman that all was well with her family and she could hear her brother's voice teasing the children. As Catherine stepped through the open door, the sight of her husband laughing heartily, with his two little girls balanced on his lap, brought a happy smile to her pale face. This did not go unnoticed by Patrick and he quickly rose to give Catherine his seat.

"Here, love. I'll pour you some tea, you look worn out. Have they been giving you extra work to do at the hotel?" he said.

"It's been busy this week, with the nice break in the weather," Catherine knew it was the encounter with Gilmore that had her visibly shaken.

"Thomas has been telling us of the strange situations he's been in on his travels across America," said Patrick. "It sounds like a grand place to raise a family. What do you think, Catherine?"

If Patrick had spoken those words at any other time, they would not have been so disturbing to his wife, but Catherine was still reeling from being trapped in a room with a man she lived in fear of. It was all too much for her and rising from her chair, she excused herself and ran towards the door. As soon as she reached the hedge at the side of the cottage,

Catherine threw up anything that was left in her stomach. It had been a long time since she had retched so violently, her last pregnancy being the occasion.

Inside the house Thomas distracted the children with a rhyming game while Lily poured some water into a cup to bring out to her sister-in-law.

"She's as white as a sheet, Patrick. I haven't heard that sound from our Catherine in a while. Not since she carried this wee mite?" Maggie tickled the child on her lap and the adults fell silent. "Well, go on out to her Lily, see what she has to say for herself."

Catherine was grateful for the cool water that soothed the sting in her throat. The retching was beginning to ease, so Lily took her by the arm and walked her to the wall that separated the garden from the road. Patrick had repaired it as best he could when they first moved in, to keep his young children from wandering off, but some of the larger stones remained lose and prone to give way. James had rebuilt it one afternoon, while Patrick was in town, and it had become a bone of contention between the two men.

"I'm much obliged to you, Lily, for your kindness," said Catherine, as she sat on the now solid wall.

"Ah sure, it's only a sup of water."

"Not just for the water. You are the only person I can talk to about what happened with Gilmore."

Catherine paused, listening to the chatter coming from inside the cottage before continuing. She told Lily about her encounter with the doctor earlier that day.

Patrick came outside, interrupting her story and the two women fell silent.

"Is there something I need to be told, Catherine?" he asked.

There was no response to his question and the young man took a few steps closer to his wife. He wanted so much to reach out and hold her but it was Lily who was comforting her. Catherine wouldn't even look him in the eye.

"Then it's true, what Maggie said."

"What did she say?" asked Catherine, jumping to her feet.

"Stop your dramatics," Patrick was getting irritated with his wife's strange behaviour. "We'll manage somehow, sure we always do. This could be a good reason to take the boat to America."

Catherine opened her mouth to speak but Lily hushed her before she could say something in haste that might be regretted later.

"Maggie thinks you might be with child, Catherine. That's what you're speaking of, is it not, Patrick?" said Lily.

"Of course it is. What else could have you in this state? Surely the opportunity of a fresh start is something to be grateful for. You have family there, Catherine. Sure, yourself and Thomas would look after us – until we get settled, wouldn't ye, Lily?" Patrick's eyes were shining with hope.

As Catherine slumped back onto the wall, she whispered something that neither Lily nor Patrick could hear. Looking up at both of them, she could see the concern on their faces.

"We didn't hear what you said, love." Patrick spoke softly.

"I said I'm not with child. I have been feeling unwell since midday. I must have eaten something that disagreed with me. It was your talk of America that upset me," Catherine's voice was not accusing, her tone as soft as Patrick's.

"I'll leave the two of you alone. You need to speak of this now, while there is no anger between you," said Lily.

Sitting by his wife's side, his arm around her shoulder, Patrick knew that whatever he said next would determine the fate of his family. It was the window of opportunity he had been waiting for and when he spoke, each carefully chosen word was heavy with emotion.

"I could go there first on my own and get work. As soon as I have enough money saved, I'll find a place for us to live, a good home for the children – not in one of those overcrowded tenements that we hear tell of. We're young and healthy, love. Now is the time to go, or we might regret it later."

Catherine looked up into Patrick's eyes. The love he had for her was plain to see and she was full of remorse for deceiving him about the circumstances of her first pregnancy. A realization came to her in a thought so clear that she knew it was the right thing to do. This, at last, was a way to repay a debt she felt was owed to her husband.

"Do you promise me that we'll come back together if it's not to our liking? You must promise me on our children's life, Patrick."

116

There was a loud whoop and Catherine found herself being picked up and swung through the air.

"I don't know what has changed your mind, and you don't have to tell me. But I want you to know that you have made me the happiest man in Ireland right now."

The whooping and laughter outside the house brought the family running through the door to see what it was all about, and Catherine nodded her approval when Patrick asked if he could tell them the news.

"Ah, I knew it. A wee brother or sister for ye, Maisie," Maggie squeezed the little girl's hand.

Patrick laughed and kissed the older woman's cheek, "You're wrong this time, Maggie. You couldn't be more wrong," he took hold of Catherine's hand. "My lovely wife here, has agreed to give America a try. As soon as I have enough to pay for my passage, I'll go over and find work. It won't be long before I have the money saved for Catherine and the wee ones to join me,"

"No, Patrick, if you go we'll be with you. We stick together in this family, is that not so, Tom?" Catherine pulled her son close. "Besides, you'd be lost without your son to mind you. You'll keep your da out of trouble won't you, my love."

CHAPTER NINETEEN

With a heavy heart Catherine listened as her father tried to console her mother. There had been no easy way to break the news of another member of their family emigrating.

"Please don't grieve so, Ma. It's only for a year, to see what it's like. Sure, you and Da did the same thing when we were children."

"A steam packet to Liverpool and a train to Sunderland is not the same as a ship to New York," James held his sobbing wife in his arms. "We will never be able to pay you a visit, and you'll not be likely to return too often, with the cost of bringing a family on such a journey. Sure how many times has Thomas come to see us, and he with a wee child here missing him sorely."

"Patrick has already agreed that we put something aside, each week, no matter how little, and so we'll have the price of a ticket for both of ye in no time. Please Da, don't make this any harder for me. We need to think of the future, for the children's sake. Can you not see that, Ma? Do ye think I'm eager to leave ye? Sure my heart is breaking at the thought of it," Catherine sat on her father's chair by the fireside and broke down.

James sat Mary on her own chair, opposite his sobbing daughter. He didn't know which one needed consoling the most. It was all he could do not to break down himself.

"Listen to me, the both of ye," he had to shout to be heard above the wailing. "Of all people, I know what it feels like to make such a grave decision, love, and we'll not hold it against you. Will we Mary?"

There was no answer from the bundle of faded black fabric rocking back and forth on the chair.

"James pulled his wife into an upright position and she clung to him. He could feel her deep sobs reverberating through her body and knew that if she didn't get a grip on her emotions, he would soon be a blubbering mass, himself.

"Now, stop your crying and let us give Catherine our blessing. We don't want to make this any harder for her than it already is, do we?" James smiled sadly at his daughter.

Catherine had a moment of weakness at the sight of tears in her father's eyes and almost changed her mind. She was not like the rest of her sisters in their longing for adventure and a new life. Breege was already saving for America and Mary-Anne would leave home at the drop of a hat. It was young Jamie that was most like her, wanting only to have his own boat one day and remain in Blackrock as a fisherman. Even he would have to accept work across the water in England, when times were lean, it was part and parcel of life in their village.

"All my children will be gone. I see it happen all the time. How many of the neighbours' grandchildren do ye see here, running around the village causing mischief? Oh what I would give to have the flowers plucked from my garden or a stone pelted at my hens by someone's misbehaving grandchild," Mary ran from the house and bumped into Patrick, who was waiting at the gate.

119

"And *you. You.*" Mary beat her son-in-law's chest with her fists. "What kind of a man takes his children away from their grandparents. Your own parents are dead, so you should be grateful that we are still here for them."

Before he could stop her, Mary ran off down the road and left Patrick feeling unsure of what he should do. He knew that she was on her way to Maggie and was thankful that his children were not in the house. Both Maisie and Tom were in school and Thomas and Lily had taken his youngest for a walk, while the news about America was being broken to Catherine's parents.

Patrick paced outside the gate, listening for any sound that might come from the house, but nothing reached his ears. That was a good sign, he thought. If James had been angry or too upset, he would have charged outside to give his son-in-law a piece of his mind. Catherine had been right in wanting to tell her parents about their decision on her own. It would not have surprise Patrick if James had followed Mary out of the house and thrown a punch at him, but that didn't happen. Instead, an eerie silence had ensued. Even the birds seemed to be silently accusing the young man of a dreadful deed. The sound of the waves breaking on the shore drew Patrick towards the village, where he hoped to find Thomas and Lily. He needed to get away from the McGrother house and its sadness.

Inside the little white-washed cottage, time seemed to stand still for James. His mind drifted to a scene in the past, when he had returned home to find his young daughter

120

trying to spoon feed her mother. Mary had been in a bad place mentally, and Catherine was trying her best to help him look after her. The scene was so vivid that for a few seconds, it was all he could see and he jumped when brought back to the present by a hand on his arm.

"Are you feeling ill, Da? I'm so sorry, I didn't think you would take it this hard," Catherine sat her father down on his chair and busied herself making some tea. "I knew that Ma would be upset, but it still hurt to see how grieved she was. Please give me your blessing, I promise I will save every farthing to bring the children home to see ye, as often as I can. Sure ye might even come for a visit yourselves. Wouldn't that be grand? Ye might like it so much that ye won't go home."

It was all James could do not to burst into tears himself, watching his eldest daughter care for him, just as she had done for her mother so long ago as a young child. He gave her a warm smile as she handed him a cup of steaming hot tea.

"Do you remember the time your ma was carrying Breege and the manner of sickness she had then?"

"I do indeed. Sure wasn't I delighted to have an excuse to stay out of school and mind her?" Catherine smiled at the memory.

"You were always a grand wee girl. Don't you go telling your sisters now, but I've always had a soft spot for you, Catherine," whispered James.

"Ah, go on with you. Sure they know that already. Haven't the two of them given me grief over it for years? We all know that you love us but when it comes to myself and Jamie there's a look you give us that's a wee bit different. Is it because we are so much like you, Da? Or because we are the first and last of your brood?"

"A bit of both, I daresay," James was beginning to feel the better for the relaxed talk and the cup of tea. "You know your ma will hold it against Patrick for taking you away don't you, love?" James said.

"Did you hear what she said to him when she ran outside?" Catherine replied as she walked to the window. "I couldn't bring myself to go out to them and I'm glad you didn't either. Ma will be with Aunt Maggie by now, crying her heart out. Patrick's gone off down the road. Poor man, he'll be wondering what you're saying to me and hoping you won't be trying to talk me out of leaving. Are you going to, Da?" she turned to face her father, "Try and talk me out of leaving?"

"No, love. I'm not. That husband of yours has a hold on you that no man could break, and that's as it should be between man and wife. But I wish with all my heart that he had left you alone, when you were in the doctor's house in England, and not gone against my wishes behind my back. You might not be thinking of America but for him. So, your ma is not the only one who puts the blame at his feet, Catherine," James gave his daughter a despondent look.

Catherine made an instant decision to tell her father part of a dreadful secret that even her husband knew nothing about. The blame that Patrick took for every calamity that befell them was unfairly put upon his shoulders. The rift between her husband and her father seemed to get wider every time they were in each other's company and nothing she could say had ever made a difference. Catherine knew that if her father truly offered his hand in genuine friendship, Patrick would put the past behind him and accept it. He was not one to bear a grudge, it was one of the traits of his character that had drawn Catherine to him.

"I was already carrying our Tom when I wed Patrick."

The words hung between them in the air, as if unsure where they should go. The ticking of the mantle clock intensified, making Catherine even more aware of the thudding of her heart.

"Did you tell me such a thing so that I might find him and kill him, and then none of ye would be sailing off to America?"

"No, Da. I told you that because we have all done Patrick a great injustice, me more so than anyone, for he is not Tom's father," Catherine slumped into her mother's chair.

Again the clock filled the silence and it seemed an age before James could bring himself to speak.

"And are you going to tell me who the father is? Or do you want me to play a guessing game with you?"

"You don't know him, Da. I don't even know who he is," Catherine was determined to keep Gilmore's identity a secret. "I was set upon on a dark evening, I never saw his face clearly. I refused to see Patrick after that even though he tried so hard to make me change my mind. I couldn't tell him what had happened, it was too awful. I let him think it was because you had forbidden us to see each other. When I found out I was with child it was Aunt Rose who talked me into marrying Patrick. She said it was for the best and that it would make him happy and give me and the child security and that nobody need ever know," Catherine broke down, no longer able to speak.

The sound of the chair scraping across the flagstone floor caused her to catch her breath and the young woman braced herself, fearing her father would strike her. Instead, she felt herself being lifted up as easily as if she was a small child and enveloped in a pair of arms even stronger than her husband's.

They stood a long time like that, father and daughter, with the clock ticking beside them and the sea breaking its waves loudly on the sand, as if it were applauding the scene taking place in the quiet house.

James brushed a strand of Catherine's hair from her face and kissed her forehead. He was filled with so many conflicting emotions, it was difficult for him to form the words of comfort he knew his daughter needed.

"We have all done a great injustice to that young man. What Rose had you do was wrong, Catherine. You could have come home to us and young Tom would have been loved just as much, father or no father."

"I know, Da. But I love Patrick with all my heart and I know it's selfish of me to say this, but if letting him think that Tom is his son allows me to spend the rest of my days with him, bearing his children, then the lie is worth it. Please don't breathe a word of this to anyone, especially not to Patrick. Promise me that you will carry this secret to your grave, as I will. I know that Rose will, too. We cannot tell a soul, promise me, Da, on Ma's life."

"You know that I'll keep your secret, I don't have to swear on anyone's life. I'm feeling bad enough about the way I've treated young Patrick that I could never bring myself to tell him the truth about his son. It would break my heart to be told such a thing about one of my own children. No, Patrick must never be told of this and as much as it grieves me to see you leave, it may be for the best. A fresh start, with Thomas and Lily to help ye settle in and keep an eye out for ye."

"What about Ma? She's in an awful state. It's the children she's hurting over more than anything. Did you hear what she said about grandchildren?" Catherine asked.

"Aye, pelting her hens and plucking her flowers. She was always one for the drama, that's where our Mary-Anne gets it from. Don't worry about your ma. I'll get her to see the sense in what ye're doing. Sure, Maggie is more than likely at that task this very minute, while drowning her in cups of strong tea." James pinched his daughter's chin between a calloused finger and thumb. "Come on now, Catherine, dry up those tears and go wash that sweet face of yours. We have a farewell party to organize for your brother and his lovely new wife. I doubt that your mother's heart will be in it, so it will be up to you and your sisters to give Maggie a hand."

Catherine hugged her father as tightly as she could and offered a silent prayer for having him in her life. Of everyone she would be leaving behind when they left Ireland, he was the one she would miss the most.

CHAPTER TWENTY

"You two are looking very serious. Has the weather being spoiling your visit home, Thomas?" asked Paddy Mac as he placed their drinks on the counter.

"I'm off back to America soon and not too happy about saying goodbye to everyone, especially my wee Eliza," replied Thomas.

"Ah, sure it won't be long before your next trip. You'll be so busy with the pace of life over there the time will have gone before you know it. Not like here, eh Patrick. If it wasn't for our Irish weather I'd be over with you looking for work myself," said Paddy Mac. "God bless the wind and rain for the business they drive through my door, is what I say."

"That's the truth of it, for sure. And here we all are like eejits, lining his pockets," one of the men at the bar remarked. "Where can a man escape to from the squabbling children and complaining wife, when he's stuck inside on a week of wet days and neither fishing nor farming to go to?"

"There's two choices. You can be up in the church, thinking and praying, or here in Paddy Mac's, drinking and swaying," said another.

The place filled with laughter and Thomas looked around at a scene he knew he would find duplicated in New York on a day just as wet and windy.

"It's the same over, only we don't have quite as many bad days in the year," he said.

"Ah well, I'll stay here so. Sure the devil you know is better than the devil you don't know.

I'm too old in the tooth to be starting over in a foreign land. Sure haven't I sons and daughters over there I can visit, if I had a mind too," Paddy Mac looked sadly at his loyal clientele. "As we all do, unfortunately."

A sad air settled on the gathering of drinkers, as they took a minute's silence in remembrance of distant loved ones.

"Well now, if that's the way ye'll be sending me off, I think I had better stay at home the evening before I go, with the squabbling children and complaining wife. I'm not sure I want to be looking at your sorry, miserable faces over my last drink in Ireland," joked Thomas.

Laughter and friendly jibing brought a smile to everyone's face and the sombre mood was lifted.

"Is there anyone in the snug, Paddy?" asked Thomas.

When told it was empty, he nodded to Patrick to follow him in, and excused himself from the crowd.

"I wanted to have a quiet word with you about Mary-Anne."

The hum of male conversation could be heard, but not loud enough to cause a distraction. Patrick was beginning to wish they were back out in the main bar, taking part in the friendly banter that the regulars at Paddy Mac's threw back and forth between each other. He was dreading whatever it was that his brother-in-law might say next.

"Look, Thomas. Whatever she's said about me isn't true. I've never done anything to make her think that I've any feelings towards her.

128

Only those of a brother of course. Even then, she's been hard to put up with these past few years, causing trouble between myself and Catherine, she's always . . ."

"Patrick, will you calm yourself down, man. I know full well the strain she's put the two of ye under. That's not what I want to speak of."

Thomas went on to tell Patrick of the scene he had witnessed in the dining room of the hotel while Mary-Anne was tending the Gilmore's table.

"I'm sure my eyes were not deceiving me when she turned around. She was enjoying every second of his attention and when she saw that I was outraged, she spoke to me as if I were a child and not her older brother."

"Mary-Anne speaks to everyone as if they were children, even your parents, Thomas. No good will come of talking to her, either. That would only make her more determined to do something foolish. I've always found it best to ignore her and Catherine has tried to do likewise. I'll be happy when we can put the Atlantic between us, for even England is not far enough away from Mary-Anne and her scheming nature."

"I might have a few words with her before I leave, not enough to make a scene, but to give her a brotherly warning about men. I cannot make my mind up if our Mary-Anne is innocent or crafty when it comes to these matters, Patrick."

"I know which one she is but I'll not say it. I don't want to cause offense. While we are here, away from the family, I would be much obliged if you could answer a few questions about New

York, Thomas. Do the Irish over there feel the same way about politics and religion as they do here?"

"Most of them do, but some have had enough of both. Why do you ask?"

Patrick knew he could speak frankly with his brother-in-law, for they had shared many a conversation over the years on such topics.

"You know well how I feel politically, but I've promised Catherine that I would not do anything to bring trouble to our door. You must remind me of this if you think I may be getting too close to any radicals. I tend to get swept up in the moment and give vent to my frustration and anger," Patrick took a long drink before continuing. "But what will hurt Catherine more than anything, is that I won't be going to Mass with herself and the children once we've settled over. I haven't told her this and I don't intend to, not while we're still here. What do you say to that, Thomas? Am I wrong to keep such a thing from my wife? Or do you think it best I tell her now, before we go?"

One look at the serious expression on Patrick's face had Thomas ready to laugh out loud. Instead, he hid his amusement behind a sympathetic smile.

"That will be the least of Catherine's worries. She will be more concerned about counting her change in a strange currency, and watching every move her children make in the street, to put too much store into a husband who refuses to accompany her to church. Granted, she'll make a fuss to begin with, but if you remain as stubborn as she does about it, she'll soon give in and respect your wishes,"

Even though they were alone in the snug, Thomas looked around before drawing close to Patrick, his voice barely above a whisper.

"You must never tell anyone what I'm about to divulge, do I have your word on it, Patrick?" he waited for a nod of affirmation. "Myself and Lily were never married by a priest. We had a civil ceremony. I couldn't bring myself to tell the family. It would break Ma's heart if she were to find out.

Patrick was stunned, "And what of Lily's family? Surely they disapproved of such a thing," he asked.

"I'm all she has, Patrick, and she feels the same as I do about religion."

"Does Catherine know about your marriage?" asked Patrick.

Thomas thought for a moment, "I doubt it, unless Lily has confided in her but I cannot see her doing so without telling me of it. And you know your wife as well as I do, Patrick. If she knows of it, Catherine would have given me a scalding by now for living in *sin* with Lily."

Patrick raised his drink and said, "Here's to your good wife, Lily. May she persuade your sister to give my soul a bit of peace, instead of always trying to save it."

Just as Thomas was about to respond, his younger brother ran through the door and leaned forward, hands on his knees, panting.

"What is it, Jamie, has someone met with an accident?" asked Thomas, jumping to his feet.

The young boy shook his head, "Not yet, but they might if you don't get back to our house this minute. Lily sent me to get the both of ye."

CHAPTER TWENTY-ONE

The sound of Patrick's youngest child crying at the top of her voice gave his legs an extra surge of power and he reached the McGrother house way ahead of the two brothers. Lily was pacing around the garden, pointing out the flowers to a very upset toddler. As soon as Ellen saw her father she wailed even louder and pulled away from Lily, stretching out her small arms to him.

"Is she hurt? Where's Catherine? Hush now, my wee angel," Patrick consoled his daughter, rocking her in his arms.

"She got a fright. I took her out as soon as I could, but it all happened so quickly. Jamie came outside with me, so I sent him to fetch you. It was Mary-Anne's fault, not Catherine's," said Lily.

Thomas and Jamie had arrived at the house and stood beside Patrick. The men waited for Lily to explain what had happened to cause Ellen so much upset. Loud voices could be heard from inside and Thomas asked if his father had returned home.

"Not yet," said Lily.

Ellen had calmed down considerably and was even giggling at Jamie's attempt to make her laugh by pulling faces at her.

Patrick kissed his little one on the forehead and held her out, "Take her for me, please, Lily. I'm putting a stop to Mary-Anne's tongue-lashing once and for all."

"I'll come with you," said Thomas. "Lily, I think it would be wise for yourself and Jamie to take Eliza for a wee walk on the beach."

Inside the cottage Mary was sitting on her chair by the fireside, rocking backwards and forwards with her head bowed. She was crying softly to herself and Thomas rushed to his mother and knelt on the floor in front of her, easing her hands from her face. The arrival of the two men brought a hush to the argument that had Mary so upset and Maggie came away from where she had been standing, in between Catherine and Mary-Anne.

"Bless us and save us, I never saw the likes of it in this house before. I thought those two were going to kill each other. Come on back to my house Mary and we'll have a nice cup of tea. I have a wee sup of whiskey we can put into it to calm our nerves," Maggie helped Thomas raise his mother to her feet.

Before the two older women had even left the house, Mary-Anne was pointing a finger at Catherine and shouting at the top of her voice. Patrick told her to calm down and settle her differences with his wife like a grown woman. He had taken Catherine in his arms, leading her to the chair that Mary had vacated, and sat her down.

"Hush now, love, and let Thomas deal with your sister," he spoke softly to his shaking wife.

"I heard that, Patrick Gallagher. No man is going to *deal* with me. I'm no longer the witless young fool who used to follow you round like a lap-dog. Do you hear? The one favour my sister did for me was to marry you and save me from the drudgery of bearing your disgusting offspring and have them hang out of my apron strings. The thought of it sickens . . ."

Thomas clamped a hand around his sister's mouth as he grabbed her from behind, stemming the flow of her venomous words.

"That's enough, Mary-Anne. *Enough*," he said, his own voice shaking with anger.

He pulled his squirming sister as far away from the young couple as the room would allow and waited until her struggling had stopped before taking his hand away from her mouth.

"You're all a bunch of cowards, do ye hear? And the biggest coward of all is my father. He could have had you run out of this village any time, Patrick Gallagher, if he'd the guts to do it?"

James stepped through the doorway and glared at Mary-Anne. The silence that fell on the room was so intense, nobody wanted to be the first to break it.

"Da, what are you doing home? Ma said you'd gone to town," said Mary-Anne in a completely calm, sweet voice.

The look on her father's face was so full of disappointment and sadness, it made the other two men in the room feel as if they were intruding and Patrick lifted his wife up to lead her outside. Thomas also began to walk towards the door.

"Stay where ye are, the three of ye. Your sister has somewhere else she'd rather be. Is that not so, Mary-Anne?" James spoke in a controlled even, tone that belied the hurt in his eyes.

"I do, as a matter of fact. I must be off back to my room at the Gilmores to pack up the rest of my belongings. I cannot say that this has been the happiest of partings, but I will miss you all, none the less. Even yourself, Patrick, even you," Mary-Anne gave a sly smile to her brother-in-law.

Catherine watched in amazement as her sister walked across the room to her father's side and stood on her toes, reaching up to kiss his cheek. James looked straight ahead, keeping his eyes averted from the other members of his family and held his breath until Mary-Anne had left the house.

"I should go after her, Da," said Catherine. "We had a disagreement and it got out of hand."

"Leave her go. Your sister has made us all perfectly aware of her feeling towards us, has she not? Patrick, I need to speak with you, alone," James turned and walked through the doorway.

"None of this was Patrick's fault, Da. He wasn't even here when it started," Catherine made an attempt to follow her father.

Patrick sat his wife back down on the chair and asked her to make some food for them all. His stomach was turning and eating was the last thing he felt like doing, but he knew the task would help to steady his wife's nerves and bring some normality back to the house. Whatever James was going to say to him, it would not change his mind about America, especially after Mary-Anne's latest attack. The more distance he could put between the two sisters, the better.

When Patrick stepped outside he saw James at the gable end of the house beckoning to him. Following his father-in-law to the back of the cottage, Patrick found him tending to the new donkey he had recently acquired, after the death of his old one. He stood beside James, stroking the animal's back.

"Did you know that Maisie asked me to call this one after herself? When I told her it was a boy, she asked me to call him after you," said James.

Patrick didn't reply, unsure where the conversation was going. He had been expecting James to blame him for Mary-Anne's outburst and was surprised at the softness in his voice.

"I've done you a great injustice, Patrick. I want to make it up to you. And to Catherine," James took an envelope from his pocket and held it out.

"What's this?" asked Patrick.

"Go on, take it. It's for you and Catherine. Put it to your savings for America, you'll need every penny you can get."

Patrick, opened the envelope and stared at the notes within.

"I cannot accept this, James. It's too much, I know by looking at it," he said. "Why are you so friendly towards me all of a sudden? Is it because I'm about to take your grandchildren away? I've already promised that I'll make sure they see you again. I don't need your money to make me keep my word on it."

James offered his hand to his bewildered son-in-law and waited for him to shake it. Patrick hesitated at first, then clasped it firmly. He could see in the older man's face an expression that had never been directed at him before, and knew instantly that something had given James McGrother a change of heart about their grievances.

"I was sure you were going to give me a piece of your mind, James. I almost walked away in the opposite direction when I followed you out of the house, it was Catherine being so upset that stopped me. I couldn't leave her here in such a state. What is it that has changed your mind about me?"

Remembering his promise to Catherine never to tell Patrick that Tom was not his son, James wanted to make sure the young man believed his friendship was genuine. He needed to convince him that he now realized the animosity he had felt towards is son-in-law was undeserved and unjust.

"It has taken me a long time to admit it, but you've been a good husband to my daughter, Patrick. And a good father to my grandchildren. What more could a man ask for? I owe you much more than a few pounds. Can you forgive me for making it so hard for you and Catherine? It was seeing what Mary-Anne has been putting you through that made me come to my senses. That and the fact that you will soon be leaving us. I don't want us to part on bad terms."

Patrick laid a hand on his father-in-law's shoulder as he placed the envelope in the inside pocket of his jacket.

"As long as you know it wasn't the money that sealed our friendship, James. I'm much obliged for it and so will Catherine be, when I tell her."

James asked him to keep it between themselves, until they were settled in their new life in America.

"You can give it to her then, Patrick. It will be a nice surprise for her when she gets there. Now, I had better go and have a word with Mary-Anne. She's another one I cannot allow to leave with such bad feelings in her heart. I know she's caused you a lot of trouble, son, but she's my flesh and blood, all the same."

Patrick had wondered why James was harnessing the donkey to the cart as they spoke.

"I'm off to fetch Mary and I fear she may not be up to much walking in the state she's in. It will break her heart to let Mary-Anne go, but she needs to say her goodbyes and I need to let her know I'll always be her father, no matter what she thinks of me."

As James led the donkey from the back of the cottage and out onto the road, Patrick remained in the garden. The envelope sat like a weight in his pocket and he was aware of a lump forming in his throat. It had taken a lot of courage for his father-in-law to admit to his faults and not let pride get the better of him. Patrick knew that he himself had not made it easy for James to make amends and as the years went by, each encounter with him had been strained and unyielding on both their parts.

"If I'm half as good a husband and father as yourself, James McGrother, I'll die a happy man," Patrick whispered.

138

CHAPTER TWENTY-TWO

Mary-Anne knew what she was doing. Mrs. Gilmore was enchanted by her and Doctor Gilmore was more attentive than ever. For a young woman who had never even courted a man, she was quickly learning how to play the game – one in which *she* made the rules. As the daughter of a fisherman she had a good knowledge of how to lure her catch, what bait to use and the best time to cast a net. Mrs. Gilmore was a very sick woman and Mary-Anne could see that the doctor had great affection for his wife. However, the poor woman had let it slip in a moment of despair over her illness, that her husband treated her like a fragile younger sister, refusing to share her bed.

If Mrs. Gilmore became pregnant one more time it would be to her detriment. She had miscarried four children already and the last one almost killed her. The couple had been warned by every consultant they had been to, that it was vital conception be avoided, at all cost. Well, it appeared to Mary-Anne that the price they had to pay was very high indeed, with her mistress crying herself to sleep most nights and the poor doctor driving himself demented. Mary-Anne knew from her own childhood that in times of famine a person would eat almost anything, what source it came from didn't matter. Mrs. Gilmore had a hunger for a child and as for her husband, he too had a craving, and neither one could satisfy the other.

Mary-Anne smiled as she waved goodbye to her family on the quayside and blew a parting kiss to her sister, Catherine, who appeared to be crying. A feeling of freedom and exhilaration shot through her body, almost lifting her off her feet. Raising herself on her toes, Mary-Anne waved a handkerchief over her head and turned to smile up at the gentleman next to her. Doctor Gilmore was gazing almost trancelike at someone below. He had a wistful expression on his face and Mary-Anne was surprised that he should feel that way about leaving Ireland. She scanned the crowded dock but could not see anyone in particular looking in his direction.

The McGrother family stood together on the quayside, and waited until the steam ship was well out into the bay. James was upset to see his wife so distraught at Mary-Anne's departure. Mary was openly weeping while clinging to her husband's arm. She wasn't sure what had hurt her the most, her daughter's eagerness to leave them, or the indifference the family had shown on hearing she would be taking the Gilmores up on their offer of permanent employment in England. It seemed strange to the distraught mother that Catherine was the only one, besides herself, to weep so bitterly as the vessel carried Mary-Anne away from them. Mary came to the conclusion that her eldest child was feeling remorse for the hostility she had recently directed towards her own sister.

Notably absent from the quayside was Patrick, who had elected to stay home with the younger children. The only two members of the McGrother family wearing genuine smiles on their faces, were young Jamie, who had never been close to Mary-Anne, and his Aunt Maggie.

The older woman's face beamed with such happiness, you would think she was welcoming the return of a loved one, instead of bidding them farewell.

Thomas and Lily remained in Dundalk while the rest of the family headed home. He didn't want their last few days in Ireland to be miserable and that's how his mother was making him feel. She was unable to hide the pain from him every time he looked at her, so Thomas had booked a hotel room in Belfast for himself and Lily that evening. He looked forward to the train journey and the opportunity to view the countryside as a tourist, passing through a landscape that no longer felt like home to him.

******

When Catherine arrived home she was surprised to find Tom and Maisie laying the table while Patrick dished up a meal he had prepared for the family. The smell of bacon made her realize how hungry she was.

"We have enough meat from our last pig to keep us going until we're ready to leave," said Patrick.

"I think we should give the wee banbh to Ma, he will be a fine sized pig by the end of the year."

"What about Maggie? Ah sure, I suppose she'll be spending most of her day with your ma, once we're gone. Did she not come back with you?" asked Patrick.

"No, Ma is in a terrible state so Maggie said she would stay with her for the rest of the day. It was awful on the journey back from town. Myself and Breege walked so that Da could drive the cart home faster and get Ma inside the house. She kept pleading with me to change my mind about America and blaming you for taking us all away," Catherine took a mouthful of food and rolled her eyes at the children. "Your Da is a good cook, isn't he? I think it's himself should stay at home and keep house, while I go out to work, once we're in America."

The children cheered as Patrick took Catherine's apron from the hook it was hanging on and tied it around his waist. Then he crossed the room to take her bonnet from the top of the dresser and when he turned around wearing it, they screeched with delight. Pulling Catherine up from her seat, Patrick told her she must learn how to lead in a waltz, if she were to be the *man* of the house. The children clapped their hands and Catherine laughed as the two of them collapsed in a tangled heap on their bed in the corner of the room.

After their meal, the young family took a long walk and ended up in Haggardstown cemetery. Catherine sat the children down by Pat and Annie's grave and talked of her childhood. She recounted amusing incidents about the elderly couple who had been like grandparents to her, and promised to tell them some of Annie's ghost stories when they were older.

Later that evening, with the children asleep in the small back room, a very contented Patrick drew his wife onto his knee as he sat by the stove he had brought from England. It had been worth forgoing the night's fishing to spend it with Catherine. He could feel how relaxed she was and he was savouring every moment of the day they had spent together.

"Should we sell the stove before we go, or give it to your Ma, along with the banbh?"

"I'd like to give it to Ma, if you don't mind, Patrick. It would make life easier for her, and Da will be happy at how much longer his sods of turf will burn for."

"Speaking of your da, he's been very friendly towards me all of a sudden. I almost fell over yesterday, when he offered me his hand and said he was sorry for misjudging me."

Catherine held her breath, worried that her father might have betrayed her confidence in some way.

"When was that? What did he say?" she asked. "What gave him the change of heart?"

"It was after your sister's outburst. He said it was Mary-Anne's behaviour that made him realize how wrong he had been to bear a grudge against me for so long and he asked me to forgive him," Patrick kissed the hand resting on his shoulder. "He meant it, too. I could see it in his eyes."

"Did you mean it when you spoke about me working, when we are settled in America, Patrick?"

"Why not? Sure you go out to work here? Mind you, I'm not staying at home, keeping house, if that's what you're thinking," he laughed.

"I wouldn't want you to. You're a grand cook, Patrick Gallagher," Catherine paused to glance over at the table, "But you're no good at cleaning up the mess you leave behind."

Patrick agreed and said if they got a maid to take care of the cleaning, then he would be delighted to stay at home and housekeep, while Catherine went off to work each morning.

"Sure, while we're at it, we might hire ourselves a butler. And a cook – that way I can spend my days at leisure. I'm sure I'll find a nice little inn to frequent while you're busy earning a wage, my love," Patrick leaned back and stretched out his arms.

"Don't forget a nanny for the children, my dear. We don't want them wearing you out now, do we? I shall want you fresh as a daisy when I come home after a hard day's work," Catherine tickled his ribs.

Patrick embraced her, pinning her arms to her sides and buried his face in her soft hair, bemoaning the fact that Maggie was not yet home. He wanted to carry his wife to their bed but feared her aunt might walk in at any minute.

"She's very late, I hope Ma is alright. Maybe I should have called to the house on the way home," Catherine's voice was filled with concern.

Fearing a cloud might descend and shatter the pleasant humour between them, Patrick assured his wife that her mother was in good hands and was probably fast asleep as they spoke

"Let's get into bed and speak some more of our new life in America," suggested Patrick.

Once they were under the covers with the curtain drawn around their bed, they reminded each other of the positive things that Thomas had told them about life in New York. He had warned them of quite a few negative aspects, too, but neither one wanted to spoil the enthusiasm of the other by mentioning them.

"Lily told me how fond the young Irish women over there are of their attire. She said they are to be seen stepping out on a Sunday morning, in the latest fashion. After they have sent money home, they seem to spend the rest on clothes and hats. Lily says my needlework would be in great demand in New York. I could start with just one customer and if she is happy with my work, then more will follow. She knows some seamstresses who work from home, as it's better than factory work and I can still keep an eye on the children. Lily says that in time I might earn a pretty penny."

Patrick was very quiet as she spoke and Catherine felt sure he'd fallen asleep.

"Well then. Do you think I might earn a pretty penny or not?"

"I think you can do anything you put your mind to, my love," he whispered. "And you can thank those *radical* meetings I attended for my change of heart about my wife taking on employment. Why, I would even encourage you to cast a vote, if that ever comes about."

"Merciful heaven, Patrick Gallagher, why on earth should I worry over political matters when I have you to do that for me?" Catherine smothered a laugh as the door creaked open.

The young couple held their breath as Maggie tip-toed across the floor in the darkness and found her way to the room she shared with the children. There wasn't a sound stirring in the house and she was sure that Patrick would have gone out in the boat that night, the weather being at its best for fishing. She didn't want to disturb Catherine, knowing how upset she had been earlier that day on the quayside in Dundalk.

"That poor girl will need her sleep tonight if she's to face her mother in the morning," sighed Maggie as she undressed. "I'm fair worn out after the drama of today, and that's a fact."

CHAPTER TWENTY-THREE

"James, my heart is breaking. I cannot stand the pain of it," Mary lay on her back, sobbing as she pounded her chest with a tightly clenched fist.

"Hush, love. You must stop all these dramatics," as he sat on the edge of the bed, James tried to pull his wife into an upright position, but she pushed his hands away.

"Don't hush me, do you hear? You could have made more of an effort to stop her. She's still too innocent to live away from her family. Something terrible is going to befall her – I can feel it in my bones," Mary sat up quickly, catching James by surprise. "You must go after her. Please, if you have any love in your heart for me, bring her home."

Mary clutched her husband's jacket and he allowed her to vent her sorrow on him, until she ran out of steam and buried her face in his chest.

"Mary-Anne is a grown woman and there's nothing I can do to stop her making her own way in the world, no more than I could stop Thomas. And it will not be long before Catherine and the children take the boat to America. We have to let them go, Mary. In time the pain will lessen and we'll come to terms with our loss."

Mary sobbed in James's arms until her energy was spent. For a long time they sat together on the edge of the bed, silently consoling each other, until James felt his wife go limp in his embrace. Realizing she had finally given in to an exhausted sleep, he gently laid her down, draping over her the patchwork quilt she had made with her daughters when they were children.

James knew how difficult it had been for Mary to put on a brave face for her family as she prepared breakfast earlier that morning. He could see in her eyes that she was being torn apart inside and prayed that she would hold out until the children had left the house for school and work. To her credit, Mary had sent them off with a smile and it wasn't until she had closed the door behind her that her breakdown had occurred. His own heart was heavy with the impending departure of his eldest daughter and her children and it was all he could do to keep control of his own emotions while he comforted his wife.

Sitting in his chair by the warmth of the fire, James reflected on how many times he must have bade farewell to family and friends from the parish over the years. He had to remind himself that both he and Mary had left Ireland themselves at one time, in search of a better life. James thought it ironic that in the end, it was back in their own village of Blackrock where they eventually found that life.

When he was younger, famine and disease were his enemies, and he fought to keep them from his door. Just when life seemed to make sense to him, the political activism of his friend, Michael Kiernan, forced James to become involved in situations he had always tried to distance himself from. The price Michael and his family paid was at a cost no one should have to bear. James lamented the fact that his son-in-law, Patrick, had been enticed into a movement that could very easily end in heartache for Catherine and her children. Even his own son, Thomas, was full of enthusiasm for radical change and although a self-proclaimed pacifist, he fought a war of words against an unjust and unequal society.

"Ah, I'm getting old and weary by the day," James spoke softly to a quiet house. "And I'm falling into the habit of talking to myself, like an old woman complaining of her ailments."

The creaking of the chair as James wearily raised himself out of it disturbed Mary and he rebuked himself for waking her from a much needed sleep. It was a pleasant surprise to see her stretch out her arms and give him a sad smile.

"Come here to me, James McGrother and let me tell you something I've been neglecting to say to a fine man such as yourself."

"Is this a trap of sorts, Mary? Am I to have my head bitten off as soon as you have me within arm's reach?"

James lay beside his wife and stroked the wisps of hair that had escaped from the tight bun she had gathered them into that morning.

"Ah, stop with your foolish talk, James. It's been too long since I last told you how much you mean to me. I'm sorry to have caused such a fuss. No doubt, I'll do it all over again when Catherine and the wee ones leave us, but as long as I still have you, I can bear it."

"You'll always have me, love. I'm staying here, no matter what happens. If we have to live in the ditch, so be it, but I fancy Maggie would come to our rescue," James started to laugh.

"Oh, we can be sure of that. Your sister has a way of turning the tables on bad luck, and that's a fact. I daresay, if the Queen herself fell on hard times, Maggie would be the best person for her to turn to. Why, she would even find her employment of some sort," Mary began to laugh, too.

Ten years appeared to fall away from her smiling face and James cupped it in his hands, drawing her lips to his. It had been a long time since either of them had been so happy in each other's company.

"I feel like a boy again, Mary. Thank you."

"And do you want me to treat you the same way as I did in our childhood, James?" Mary pulled away, prudishly. "If so, I must ask you to leave my bed this instant. But if you were to feel more like the young man that I married, then I might be tempted to behave differently."

James smiled and drew her close, her teasing assuring him that she was still the wife he had come to love and cherish so much. At that moment, in spite of their heartbreak and sorrow, James knew they were bound together by more than love or family. Every fibre in his being connected him to Mary with an invisible chord that even death would find impossible to sever.

CHAPTER TWENTY-FOUR

The stooped figure of her mother, bending over a wooden pen as she fed two noisy piglets, brought a tear to Catherine's eye. She quickly gathered herself together and wiped the salty drop away, before it could be seen.

"Ma, Breege says you wanted to see me, out here in the garden."

Mary placed the empty bucket on the ground beside her and slowly turned to face her eldest child. The two women held each other's gaze until Catherine noticed one of Aunt Annie's wooden bowls in her mother's hand.

"I want you to take this with you, to America. I've given one to Thomas, but I asked him not to tell any of ye before he left. I wanted to surprise you with one of your own," Mary held out the shiny wooden bowl that had been passed down to her by James's aunt. "I never thought to give one to Mary-Anne and I regret that now, but sure I'll see her soon enough, no doubt. She won't stay away for too long."

"Ma, you cannot split up the set like this. These are yours and they must stay in Ireland, in your home," Catherine's eyes glistened.

"Myself and your da have always agreed that each of our children should get one of these after we're gone," Mary stepped forward and placed the bowl in Catherine's shaking hands. "We may not be gone yet, but our children are leaving us, one by one."

"Oh Ma. Please don't make this any harder for me than it already is."

Mary wiped Catherine's face with the end of her apron and shook her head slowly, "There's no easy way to say farewell, you know that yourself, my love. Tomorrow your da will bring you and the children to take the boat to Liverpool, but I'll be staying here. Don't ask me to be there when you leave, I've stood on that dock too many times, watching those I care about sail out of my life. I cannot do it again after what happened over Mary-Anne. It almost killed me. That's why I couldn't go to see Thomas and Lily off."

"So you were not ailing the day they left, were you, Ma?"

"It was my heart that was troubling me, love, not my stomach," Mary turned to look at the pen where the piglets were still rummaging through the scraps. "It was very good of you to give us your banbh, Catherine, and your stove. You should have sold them both to raise a bit more money for America."

Catherine assured her mother that they had enough to keep them going until Patrick found work. Thomas and Lily had moved to a larger apartment on their return to New York and had invited the young family to stay with them for as long as they wished.

"Now my love, let's wipe our eyes and go back in to the family, they'll be starving waiting for us to join them. We should make this last meal together a happy memory for the wee ones to carry away with them," said Mary.

When Catherine and Patrick left the house later that evening, Mary said her final farewell and asked them not to call to see her on the way to the boat next day. She kissed each of the children and told them that it wouldn't be long before they saw one another again and that they must gather a book-full of stories about their adventures in America.

"I'll want to hear about everything ye've been getting up to. Do ye hear me now? The good as well as the bad, and I promise I won't tell your da," Mary winked at Patrick.

As she kissed her son-in-law's cheek, she whispered in his ear that if anything should happen to her grandchildren or her daughter, she would hold him personally responsible and never forgive him.

"I give you all my blessing on your new life," Mary said dry-eyed, smiling at each one of them, including Patrick. "But if America is not for ye, then come home. There'll be no shame in it. Some do come back, you know."

Mary opened the door and shooed them all outside, including Maggie. "Now go on, the lot of you. I can't stand around here gabbing all day. There's work to be done, is that not so, James?"

******

The next day both Patrick and Catherine were relieved that Mary had said her goodbyes already and that the heart-breaking scene that occurred at Mary-Anne's departure, would not be repeated. Only the young ones chatted to each other as the men silently walked each side of the donkey leading the cart to Dundalk. Maggie was sitting with the children, pointing out to them the Cooley Mountains and other landmarks they were to bring to mind when living far from home.

James looked over the donkey's head at his son-in-law and made an attempt at some small talk, but neither of them were in the form for conversation. When they arrived at the quayside Catherine asked to speak to her father alone and took him to one side.

"I know why Jamie didn't come with us. He's at home with Ma, isn't he? You were worried about her being left alone."

James smiled at his daughter, who had always been so tuned in to his feelings, even as a little girl.

"He is and I was. I gave him a bit of work to do until I get back, so your ma would not send him off out of her way. Don't be worrying about her, Catherine. She'll be fine once Maggie moves in with us."

"Breege is planning on leaving, too. You know that don't you, Da?" Catherine's face was creased with worry.

"Of all of you, our Breege is the one we both knew would follow Thomas to America. Sure hasn't she been warning us about that for years now," James replied, smiling.

He cupped his hands around Catherine's head and gently massaged her forehead with his thumbs.

"I don't like to see those worry-lines on that pretty face of yours, so give your old da a big smile. That's better. That's the picture I'll carry in my head on the way back home to your ma."

Catherine turned to look at Patrick, who was standing with young Tom and pointing out something on the steam packet ship they would soon board.

"At first, I only agreed to go to America because I owed it to Patrick. But now, I really do want to make a new life for us there," Catherine's eyes lingered on her eldest child. "If I stay here, all I will have to pass on to my children will be a legacy of secrets. I want to end my days, knowing I've done the best I can for them, and for Patrick. Can you understand that, Da?"

"I can indeed, love. Why do you think we came back here to Ireland? I had regular work in England and we had a decent roof over our heads, but your ma and myself decided that our children would have a better life here, in Blackrock. The thought of getting back into a boat was tempting, I'll admit, and made it easier for me to come home. But we both felt sure in our hearts that it was the best decision for the family."

"And it was, Da. It was. If you ever doubt that, just take a look at Jamie's face when he's preparing to go out in the boat. He's the spit of yourself, inside and out and I know, for sure, he'll never leave home. You must remind Ma of that when she's missing the rest of us," said Catherine.

"Aye, I'll do that, love. Now, I had better leave you off to gather yourselves together, you'll be boarding soon," James embraced his daughter one last time. "I'll not stay to see ye off. Maggie says she would rather leave before the boat does and I'm inclined to feel the same way."

While Catherine and her aunt embraced and dabbed tears from each other's cheeks, James took Patrick out of earshot of the women.

155

"We'll not be staying, son. I think it best we get back to Mary, she's very low in spirit right now."

Patrick held out a hand to his father-in-law, "I'm sorry to have caused so much trouble. I feel bad about taking the family so far away from ye."

James took a hold of the younger man's hand, shaking it firmly as he placed an arm around Patrick's shoulder.

"There's no need for apologies. The past is behind us, it's what's ahead we need to think on. I've told you before, I couldn't have asked for a more decent man than yourself as a father to my grandchildren and I know you'll do right by Catherine. Try not to get into any trouble with those radicals over there, you've to set a good example for that fine son of yours. You do that, and I'll be a happier man for it."

Patrick nodded his head and picked up Maisie, who had come running over to them. James leaned in to kiss her cheek and put some coins in her palm. "Buy a few sweets when you get to Liverpool, Maisie love. For the three of ye, mind. Else you'll give yourself a belly-ache."

"I will Dadó."

"Tell your dadó how much you love him, Maisie," said Patrick.

"I love you more than the banbh, Dadó," she leaned in and kissed her grandfather's whiskered cheek.

The two men laughed and Maisie joined in, her face beaming with delight.

James touched the side of his face, where the gentle kiss had been planted and felt his heart skip a beat. He caught Maggie's eye and pointed towards the cart. It was becoming more difficult for him to keep the smile on his face and he knew the same was probably true for his sister.

After another round of farewells James and Maggie left the quayside, turning to wave one last time at their little family before disappearing from view.

Catherine slipped her hand into Patrick's and sighed. Saying goodbye to her father had not been as distressing for her as she had expected. It wasn't that her love for him had diminished in any way, it was just that her husband had finally taken his rightful position in her heart. Patrick squeezed her hand reassuringly.

"We'll be grand, love. I promised your da I'd do right by ye and I'm a man of my word, you know that, don't you?"

"I do, Patrick," Catherine replied, her eyes lingering on the spot where her father had waved his last farewell to them. "Of course we'll be grand, sure Da gave us his blessing, didn't he?"

THE END

<u>Book Five to follow in 2016</u>

References

Chapter Four

<u>Susan Brownell Anthony</u> (February 15, 1820 – March 13, 1906) was an American social reformer and feminist who played a pivotal role in the women's suffrage movement. Born into a Quaker family committed to social equality, she collected anti-slavery petitions at the age of 17. In 1856, she became the New York state agent for the American Anti-Slavery Society.

In 1872, Anthony was arrested for voting in her hometown of Rochester, New York, and convicted in a widely publicized trial. Although she refused to pay the fine, the authorities declined to take further action. In 1878, Susan Anthony along with life-long friend, Elizabeth Cady Stanton, arranged for Congress to be presented with an amendment giving women the right to vote. Popularly known as the Anthony Amendment, it became the Nineteenth Amendment to the U.S. Constitution in 1920.

https://en.wikipedia.org/wiki/Susan_B._Anthony

Chapter Eleven

<u>The International Workingmen's Association</u> (IWA, 1864–1876), was also known as the First International. It served to unite a variety of different left-wing socialist, communist and anarchist political groups and trade unions that grew out of the struggles of the working class. In Europe there had been a backlash from the ruling class to the widespread Revolutions of

1848. The next major revolutionary activity began nearly twenty years later, when the International Working Men's Association was founded in 1864 at a meeting that took place in Saint Martin's Hall, London. Its first congress was held in 1866 in Geneva.
http://www.wsm.ie/story/1778?page=1

Chapter Twenty-Two

Banbh is the Irish word for a piglet, pronounced *bonniv.*

Acknowledgements

I'm extremely grateful for and very much appreciate the feedback my beta readers gave on *A Legacy of Secrets*. Their input was both helpful and encouraging. Many thanks to Brenda, Diane, Ellen, Vera, Eileen, Alan, Patricia and Dana. Here's to the next book in the saga.

Also, a big thank you goes out to poet Noel Sharkey, author Oliver Murphy, Jacintha Matthews and team of Dundalk FM 100 literary program *The Creative Flow*. Last but not least, many thanks to the *Sixty Minutes Show* host, Pat Carroll and his colleagues of Youghal's local radio CRY 104 FM. You've all played a huge part in encouraging me.

A special mention must go to my grandson, Ethan, whose image is on the front cover of the book, and to my mother, whose faith in me never waivers, no matter how much I doubt myself.

Also, this printed version would never have been possible without Bob Reinhardt's help with the formatting. Fortunately, I didn't have to pay him as I'm his wife.

Last but not least, a very big 'THANK YOU' to all you lovely readers who have joined me on this journey of words and make it so worthwhile.

15125111R00096

Printed in Great Britain
by Amazon.co.uk, Ltd.,
Marston Gate.